EYES OF A CHILD

EYES OF A CHILD

James Haddad

|CB|
COMMONWEALTH BOOKS INC. NEW YORK 1999

A Commonwealth Publications Paperback
EYES OF A CHILD
This edition published 1999
by Commonwealth Books
All rights reserved

Copyright c 1997 by James Haddad
Published in the United States by Commonwealth Books Inc., New York,
and simultaneously in Canada by Commonwealth Books of Canada,
Alberta.

Distributed by Ingram Book Company
One Ingram Blvd. P.O. Box 3006
La Vergne, TN 37086-1986
(615) 793-5000

Library of Congress
Cataloging-in-Publication Data

Haddad, James.
Eyes of a Child : a novel / by James Haddad
1st ed.
Library of Congress Catalog Card Number : 98-74720

ISBN: 1-892986-00-0

No part of this book may be reproduced or utilized in any form or by
any means, electronic or mechanical, including photocopying, recording,
or by any information storage and retrieval system, without permission
in writing from the publisher.

This work is a novel and any similarity to actual persons or events is
purely coincidental.

Manufactured in the United States of America

For Denise Khoudary–

A wonderful person and true friend whose kindness and compassion, dedication and rare qualities with children are indispensable and greatly admired.

Acknowledgments

A thanks to Paul for helping me create the idea and protagonist. Thanks to Dr. Richard Sugg and Dr. Charles Elkins of Florida International University both of whom taught me how to write. And a final and utmost thanks to Dr. E. Ted Gladue who, on a daily basis for two years, gave me the incentive and encouragement needed to complete this book.

Author's note

There are many books out there today containing the phrase(s), "Eyes of a Child." There is even a novel out there with that exact title. Even the media has incorporated this phrase and has used it continuously. The movie "Cops" even presented an hour show with the title, "Eyes of a Child."

Additionally, there are scores of novels out there today containing plots with a female child abuser abusing a little girl. This type of plot seems to be commonplace among many writers today. It seemed to have gained popularity in the early nineties and is still going strong.

However, the phrase and setting containing a female child abuser was actually invented in 1983 when I constructed my novel, "Eyes of a Child."

I am delighted to announce that I am the originator of the phrase and idea of the female child abuser. I am also flattered that many writers have found my work enticing enough to mimic me.

And now I present the original, "Eyes of a child."

EYES OF A CHILD

Anxious days and troubled nights....

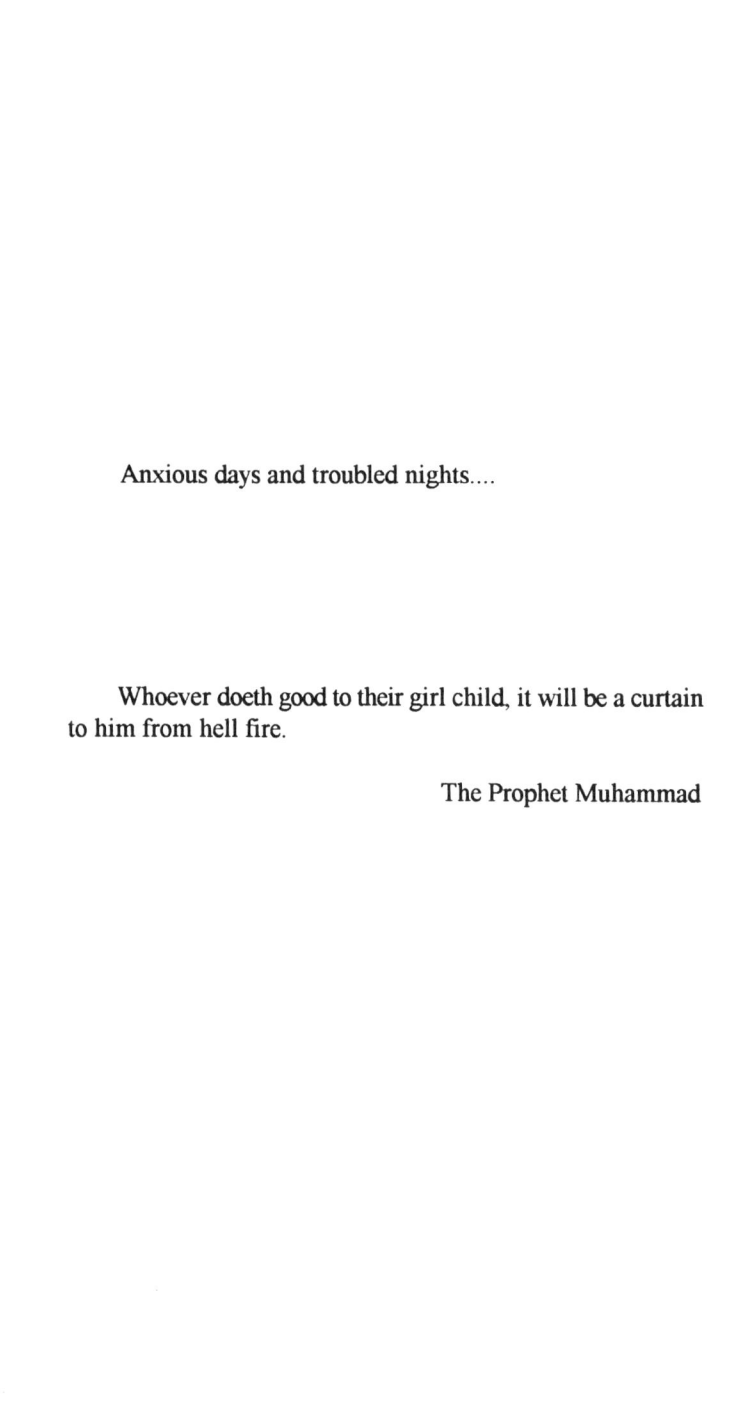

Whoever doeth good to their girl child, it will be a curtain to him from hell fire.

The Prophet Muhammad

Preface

I am dead. I speak out from my grave. Every year, hundreds of children are brutally killed by their parents; some of the deaths are unavoidable. Believe me, I know, because my mother killed me. I don't blame my mother for my death though. I blame a faulty child protective system for not doing its job.

I don't really hate my mother either. But I do hate society for letting my life be taken. Oh, how society betrayed me! Years before my death I suffered terrible pain and injury at my mother's hands, and nobody came to save me. I don't feel sorry for myself because I was killed. But I cry when I recall that I was so small and helpless, like millions of other kids, and our dependency for existence had made us potential victims of adults. I realize that child abuse and maltreatment will be with us until we reorder our social priorities.

However, many abused children, perhaps three quarters of them, could be saved by an effective and efficient child protective system. The system may not be able to prevent the fundamental causes of abuse, but once abuse is discovered in a family, the system should be able to prevent future abuse by protective social action or removal of the child. There is no such system today.

According to conventional wisdom, the failure of our

institutions is caused by a dreadful lack of facilities, social workers, judges, shelters, and of all sorts of rehabilitative social and psychiatric services. Undoubtedly, if we poured more money into existing facilities and services, if properly utilized, could go a long way toward filling the need for service. In fact, unless existing services are first put into order, additional money could not be properly utilized. Most states have expensive, mismanaged or unmanageable child welfare systems that do not fulfill the important child protection responsibilities assigned to them.

Generalizations are always unfair, and it is true that there are many judges, attorneys, probation officers, social workers and clerks who are vitally dedicated to the children and families involved in the court process. However, they are a minority, and the constant demoralization they face discourages many of them. It is hard to convey the sense of dehumanization and frustration engendered by the present system. It is not only the child who is caught up in the largely futile process. Every person in the system works with the knowledge that he is most often helpless in meeting the needs of those that come before him. Our child protection system is a fraud.

The illusion of help misleads the public. The plight of the kids, the victims of deprivation and attack, must be exposed in all its grim reality. Only in that way will society demand that these kids receive the protection they deserve.

But if humanitarian feelings cannot mobilize sufficient resources to really help the kids, perhaps a consideration of the social costs in failing to provide sufficient care will. Society tends to think of abused and neglected children as only injured physically, but the emotional damage may be equally severe and may have more long-lasting consequences. Professionals agree that such children have extremely high potential to engage in socially deviant and criminal acts. Unless the cycle of child abuse is broken, the social deviance that is its heritage shall recur. Abuse turns the child toward aggression, violence, and crime. We must break this vicious cycle. The abuse and neglect of children must be recognized as a major factor in the production of criminals. There is an urgent need to treat such children before they become the criminals of tomorrow.

From my point of view, it is less expensive to protect and rehabilitate a child then it is to endure the social costs of his later deviant behavior.

Chapter One

She was drenched in a flood of anxiety as her mother grabbed her angrily by the hair, with a violence that almost pulled her hair out by its roots. Yanking viciously on her hair, her mother jerked her head sideways, almost breaking her tiny neck. With another yank, she was thrown to her knees with a sickening groan, and she screamed out with a horrified cry:

"Mom, please don't hurt me again!"

"It's your own damn fault," she ignored her terror, tearing off Lena's dirty shirt. "You've made a mess again." Her temper flared; she folder her fist so tight, her knuckles seemed to glow. "You're just like your father."

Lena shivered like a leaf, knowing what her mother had in mind. She tried to run, but her legs seemed glued in place. Her mouth opened in a silent scream when the fist lashed out, stopping short of punching out her teeth. Lena jerked her hands up dreadfully to shield her mouth from another possible punch.

The mother hovered over her terrified child. "I ought to kill you."

"Please don't," she pleaded.

"Next time you make a mess I'm gonna hurt you, bad." Her tone was laden with danger. "Real bad!" she screamed at her daughter who nodded in agreement with a puzzled, terrified gaze.

Lena shivered uncontrollably, almost gagging on her very

EYES OF A CHILD   11

breath. Sure, Mommy, she pledged in silence, you'll never see me make a mess again, and I do mean never again. I don't want my teeth knocked out. I like bubble gum too much.

The mother quietly relented and Lena overcame her dread with deep relief, watching her mother slowly retreating away from her. Then her mother stopped to Lena's distress.

"Mom, I want my Dadee!" she called nervously, fearfully.

"Why, Lena?"

"I just want my Dadee." Her father always treated her nice.

"He'll be home soon enough."

"Why does he work so much?"

"He doesn't like being around the house."

"Why doesn't he like being around the house?" Lena knew the problem was her mother, not the house.

"He thinks he's too good for that."

"Does he work hard, Mom?"

"Not at all; he just goes to work, hangs around until he's tired of hanging around, then he comes home."

"Then after he comes home, you and him only fight?"

"You got it right." Her mother groaned. "I've got work to do, Lena."

Her mother grumbled and started for the kitchen.

"Mom, what does Dadee do at work?"

"Not a damn thing that I know of." Her mother sounded angrier than before.

"Really, Mom?"

"I'd never lie to you. I'm your mother."

She saw her mother starting back toward her with a dangerous glint in her eyes and Lena gasped.

"Stop bothering me," she suddenly burst into tears. "He doesn't love you, only Mommy does."

Out of fear and confusion, Lena cried too. Her mother

suddenly looked guilt stricken. She stopped abruptly, turned, and knelt to kiss her daughter on the forehead.

"I'm sorry, Angel," her mother apologized, tears staining her face. "You'll be awright."

"I hope so," Lena's voice crackled.

Her mother walked off and Lena's anxiety rapidly faded. Lena stirred about the filthy wooden shack, eating cereal, playing with her toys, and contemplating how her mother regarded her father as being mean, lazy, crazy, and always up to no good; the only way she had ever visualized her father showed him as friendly, happy, always playful, and avoiding arguments. Steadily, she grew tired and finally climbed upon the living room couch. She stretched her arms as she lay down, hearing the hum of a fly in the humid gloominess. Within minutes she dozed off to sleep and dreamed that there was a dark, ugly creature lumbering her way holding a cup of scalding coffee, preparing to throw it on her. Oh, oh, she had better run and hide before she got burnt....

She jumped off the couch and tried to hide underneath but she would not fit. On all fours she darted for the kitchen to seek refuge by her mother, and as she reached the slimy floor she saw DJ, the skinny kid who often visited her, and who was her best friend. DJ held a cup of coffee to his lips and asked, "Lena, why are you running?"

"I don't wanna get burned, DJ!"

"Nobody would burn a pretty little girl of four," DJ said, sipping his coffee and looking away from Lena as there came an eerie groan.

BAAAAA! the creature was almost upon them, but Lena believed him and said: "Awright!" and she turned away from DJ only to find that it was not an ugly creature, but her mother who held the cup of scalding coffee. She wanted to run and hide but her dread had turned her legs into stumps of lead. Then her mother splashed the coffee against her little chest, burning off an oblong patch of flesh. She was unable to scream and unable to move and she realized that her mother had burned her as cruelly as she had always wanted to burn her father. Her mother was moving toward her again with those luminescent green eyes filled with hate, and finally Lena let out a morbid scream. She could sense her mother was delighting in pouring hot coffee on her...BAAAAAH...

She jolted awake, sensing the taste of dread in her mouth.
"Lena!"
Darkness was showing behind windowpanes and she thought her mother was drinking a cup of coffee.
"Are you awake? Your Daddy's home. He just pulled into the yard."
Her adrenaline was pumping as she sat up nervously, fearing that her mother had scalding coffee to throw on her.
"Open the door for 'im. If you want."
"Awright," she answered with a cute smile.
She slid to the floor and her little legs, tingling with needles, led her stumblingly across the dirty carpet to the mildewed windowpane. Squinting, she peered out and was happy to see the headlights coming to her. Slumber was about to overwhelm her as she yawned, staring sleepily out the window. Her mother was close behind her.
"Lena."
She responded obediently. "Huh?"
"Open the door for Daddy."
Fighting off her sleepiness, she moved to the door and wanted to open it. But where on the door was the knob? She let her hands move aimlessly against the door. Then with a stroke of luck, her hands clutched the doorknob. She started twisting on the doorknob, but when she tried to pull the door open, it would not budge. When she heard her father's footsteps on the porch, she released her grip on the knob and called for help.

"Mom. The door won't open."

She turned around and looked up; her mother was still close behind her, with her hands on her hips.

"Open the door."

Oh, Mommy wanted to see her do it! Wanting to please Mommy, she gripped the doorknob and started twisting on the slippery, cold knob. But the door still would not budge.

"I can't do it," she almost cried.

"I'll get it," her mother said.

"Awright." She felt better.

Waiting, absorbed in glee, she stared at her mother who unfastened the lock, then turned and disappeared, her bare feet swishing toward the bedroom. Blinking wide awake now, Lena threw back the wooden door just as her father opened the screen door and smiled down at her holding a bag.

"There's my baby!" her father greeted her. He laid the bag down upon a pile of dirty clothes lying on the floor and picked her up with one arm and kissed both her cheeks affectionately.

"Kiss, Dadee," she squealed, feeling secure in her father's muscled arms. "You bring me something?"

"Like always." He eyed the plastic bag lying on the clothes.

She twisted out of his arms and when she crept toward it she noticed pink fur at the opening of the bag, then she sensed it was a stuffed animal.

"It's all yours," her father said.

She took a curious look at the fluffy lacing; it looked alive and slippery and she giggled, squealingly.

"It's real," she purred.

"It's dead as hell," her mother interrupted.

"Don't say that," her father scolded, taking the stuffed animal and stroking its velvety fur. "See. It's not real and it's not dead, hon."

EYES OF A CHILD   15

"Are you sure." Suspicion gilded her eyes now. "Does it bite?"

"Of course not." Her father looked annoyed. "It's only a stuffed Easter bunny."

"It looks so real..." Her mood suddenly changed.

Her suspicious probing mind wandered then dwelled uncertainly on her mother, for that awful dream was still at the front of her consciousness.

"He doesn't bite, Mommy," Lena told her.

The little girl's father watched Lena cuddle the floppy-eared Easter bunny, stroke the fur, hug it, then take another wary look at her mother.

"Something going on that I don't know about?" he asked Lena's mother.

"Not that I know of," her mother responded meanly.

Her mother lashed out rudely at the bunny's ears and ripped out a bunch of pink fur.

"Lena, I think your mother wants to ruin your stuffed bunny." Her father extended his hand as if asking for the bunny rabbit. "Well, if she doesn't want you to have it I'll just take it back."

"No, Dadee." Her gleaming hazel eyes lost a little luster. Her father leaned up against the living room wall and folded his arms, and naturally his biceps bulged, waiting patiently for her mother's reaction. He seemed to accept her full minute of silence as approval in allowing Lena to keep the bunny rabbit.

"I wanna keep 'im," Lena said wholeheartedly.

"Okay." He gave her the plastic bag.

"What's this for, Dadee?"

"To keep it nice and pretty till Easter's here," her father told her. "It ain't but a couple days..."

She crushed the bunny rabbit to her chest and smiled, wrinkling her eyebrows at the whiskers, its pink fur looking pinker next to her rosy cheeks.

"Yippee," she squealed. "I've got an Easter bunny!" She kept hugging the bunny. "I'm gonna give 'im a name too," she giggled, folding the bag and holding securely onto it. Drenched with glee, she flashed her tiny brown teeth. "He's all mine," she boasted to her parents.

Her mother grumbled and headed for the bedroom. The door banged shut.

Lena's happiness vanished but still she expressed her gratitude for having the toy.

"Thank you for the bunny rabbit," she said.

"You're welcome, hon," her father said.

"Why are you and Mommy alway talkin' bad?" Lena asked him. "And how come she tried to rip off my bunny's ears?"

"Some people are just mean," he explained and slowly walked away.

To Lena there hovered a vague understanding of her parents' perpetual bickering.

"Why are some people just mean, Dadee?" she called anxiously without really understanding her question.

"Because misery loves misery," his voice echoed in finality.

She gradually absorbed the troubled look on her father's face, and hugging her bunny, she went to her room, whimpering, trembling, filled with uncertainty. At about midnight, when her father was sound asleep, Lena threw her bunny rabbit to the floor and stomped all over its face; even pulled on its ears. For a whole week she refused to name her Easter bunny and, shortly after, lost her desire for it altogether.

Chapter Two

Lena came toward her mother in an act of opposition and she walked very timidly, scraping her hands against stucco walls, summoning ways to feel strong and confident. Her mother was seated at the cluttered kitchen table, chain smoking, sipping coffee, her face two inches away from a clumsy television that blared ridiculously. If her mother was not watching a soap opera then it was a horror movie. She bet Mommy was going to be angry when she realized Lena came to confront her for her hostility toward her father. Lena's timidness left as she was beginning to get irritated with the noisy television when her mother pulled off her TV eyeglasses to greet her.

"Good morning, Angel."

She stared, thinking, analyzing her mother, who did not wait for a return greeting and quickly returned to her horror movie and started ignoring her. As the TV still roared with screams and shouts of unfortunate victims of blood sucking vampires, it started straining Lena's nerves.

"Where's Dadee, Mommy?" she asked politely.

"Gone as usual, Angel," her mother reached out her arms. "I told you he was no good."

"No," she whined, throwing a tantrum.

She was scared. Should she go back to her room? Or should she cry so Mommy would be nice. Her mother had used the bunny rabbit as a way to oppose her father and she resented this. Now, as she stood glaring at her mother, it felt soothing to oppose her. Her mother's arms slowly fell to her sides; she glared for several more seconds, then she exploded, fuming, stamping her tiny, bare feet.

"No. You're bad. Bad."

In a flash her mother had lashed at her and yanked brutally on her hair. She fought back, intensely pleased with her opposition. Lena's defiance of her mother was justified in her eyes.

"Stop, Mommy. Don't break my neck."

"I couldn't do that, everybody would find out," her mother said, slapping her for a final time, then slamming her into a chair beside the television set.

She was about to run off, but her mother's palm knocked her back into her seat and the stars sparkled before her eyes.

"Let me go."

"Why should I? Maybe I should beat you more," her mother said in a mean voice charged with anger.

"Maybe I should beat you to death like Baby Lollipop's mother did to him. You would be better off. Then I wouldn't have you to bother me."

That upset Lena more. Her mother gripped her hair again, and practically dragged her out of the kitchen where she suddenly pushed her to the floor like a bundle of dirty diapers. Expecting the worse, she fearfully studied her mother's glaring green eyes, her cold hateful face, the straggly unkempt hair that touched her shoulders. She had never been able to understand her mother who seemed like a stoic, brutal stranger whose mood swings could be really dangerous.

"What's goin' on, Lena?" her mother asked in disbelief since Lena never acted this way before.

"You've been mean to me," Lena said. "You've been mean to Dadee too." Her voice sounded sad and tears came to her eyes. "You hurt my bunny rabbit, Mommy."

Lena misunderstood an uncertain personality that scared her. Now expecting more harsh treatment she felt it wise to start crying.

"It's your daddy who's bad, Lena."

"Huh uh, Mommy," she gasped.

"Don't huh uh me," her mother said.

"You're bad," Lena mumbled.

"You wanna come watch TV with me, Angel?" her mother changed suddenly, unexpectedly.

"Nooo," Lena whined

"Whatever."

Her mother then yanked several times on Lena's hair.

"You're hurtin' me," she cried. "How would you like for me to pull your hair?"

"I don't know why I birthed you," her mother groaned, releasing her hair.

The released hair eased her sad little sobs. She stopped crying altogether when her mother sat back at the table, because whenever her mother watched her horror movies, she never yanked on her hair. Lena was unable to grasp what her mother had meant about birthing her and understood nothing of her mother's mercurial personality. A clear thick liquid trickled from her nostrils to her rosy lips, and she unconsciously licked at it.

"Why do you do that?" her mother screamed.

"Because," she whimpered and licked again.

"You're disgusting," her mother complained.

Her mother rose from the table as Lena glimpsed the TV just as a vampire sucked the blood from a beautiful blond woman's neck; she took a stinky towel that she threw at her. Lena picked it up carefully with two fingers and knew what she was supposed to do, but did not want to obey, or get that filthy rag too close to her face. Then, after a moment's hesitation, she succumbed in obedience. Her left hand seemed to cramp as she wiped her nose and she felt she was going to vomit from the odor.

"Angel," her mother said as sweet as she could, "you want breakfast?"

Lena let the rag fall to the floor; her misty eyes blurred her vision; she shrugged her shoulders in a silly way, hoping to torment her mother as her mother tormented her and her father.

Her mother emerged from the kitchen and stared hard and strangely at Lena.

"I ain't hungry," Lena spoke first.

"Get to the table," her mother fumed.

"But I ain't hungry."

"Don't play with me, or I'll pull every hair out of your head," her mother warned. "Your father is at fault for your bothering me. You see how bad he treats me and that makes you treat me bad. Everything was fine until you were born. Get to the table, now.

Lena remained totally immobile as if she was a four-year-old mannequin.

"Didn't you hear me?"

"Yeah," she whispered.

"Then get to the table." Then to Lena's surprise her mother changed tactics just as she thought she had a fetish for pulling out hair. Her mother grabbed her by the ear, pinched it real hard, then led her to the table. "You like to be treated like that?"

"No," she whined to Mommy's disappointment, feeling defeated and worthless and her mother's fingernails pinching her ear.

"You're as bad as your dad."

"He ain't bad."

"If he wasn't he wouldn't have taught you by example to

EYES OF A CHILD   21

bother me." The plates and silverware tinkled as her mother complained while setting breakfast for her.

Lena had no appetite and merely picked at the hard boiled egg, sipped at the cup of Coke, and only stared at half of a chocolate Easter bunny which her mother had set before her. Today breakfast seemed just a little too sweet for her. She knew Easter was right around the corner, but a half-pound of chocolate bunny rabbit was just a little too generous. She had to dispose of it some way to please her mother since she could not eat it. Moments later she stirred the remnants of her egg in with her soda, then pushed the plastic cup off the table and watched the cup and contents bounce all over the floor.

"I'm all through, Mommy!" Lena exclaimed.

"Good girl," her mother boasted, almost slipping on the mess. Then she grew angry. "I could have broke my neck, Lena." Good, Lena thought maybe it will put some sense into you.

Boldly, and as her mother turned her back, she gripped the chocolate bunny and threw it across the kitchen, watching the soft, dark chunk roll and finally stop in the middle of the living room floor.

"Lena," her mother yelled, accidentally stepping on the chocolate before putting it back into the refrigerator to feed to Lena later.

"Huh?"

"That's bad," her mother said. "Did your father teach you to do that? Don't ever do it again."

"Awright," Lena consented.

Lena looked around the nasty kitchen. Soiled dishes crawling with roaches were piled everywhere. Soiled dishes were on the table, around the sink, and in the sink. Stacks of soiled dishes were even piled on the floor. A swarm of gnats swirled around the soiled dishes.

Disgusted, Lena covered her eyes and wished that when

she uncovered them she would just be awakening from an unpleasant dream.

"What now, Lena?" her mother yelled. "What am I going to do with you?"

She uncovered her eyes and saw her mother holding the same filthy rag on which she wiped her nose and, to her despair, it was not a dream. Her mother's eyes were glaring with madness.

"If you don't want me to kill you, you better get away from me!"

"Awright," Lena sighed. She twisted from her chair and slid to the floor. Cat-like, she picked her way over the dirty dishes, the mess she made, broken ceramics, toys and garbage. As she played in the living room she could hear her mother working in a kitchen that never got cleaned. Excitement engulfed her as she thought of going outdoors. Going to the front door, she stared out into the pale yellow morning where a gentle breeze swept through the trees. She opened the door, trembling in excitement that she was really going outside all by herself. Then she jolted and stopped, seeing a kid motioning for her.

"Hi, Lena."

It was her best friend, DJ. Around him were other neighborhood kids, playing in the heat.

"You wanna play with us, Lena?" DJ asked.

"Sure," Lena said, her eyes shining in glee.

She took a quick glance back into the house. Her mother would not miss her if she slipped out for a while. After all, her mother told her to get away from her. Lena walked across the yard and stopped at the edge of the road to look both ways. A car suddenly swerved and there came a rumbling sound of debris and gravel as a speeding car seemed to lose control, almost hitting her. She screamed, gasping, trembling. The car slowed down a lot and a cruel clump of faces stared. Then the driver slammed his hands against the steering wheel and holleered.

"Get away from the road, stupid, before you get run over!"

They better get off that dope, she thought.

She did not say it; it was terrible, that word "dope"; she had used it before and her father had yelled at her until she promised she would never deal with dope's who used dope.

She looked at the car, then at DJ and his friends whose mouths hung open in awe. She gasped deeply, then retreated further into the yard. A few feet later she stopped, foreboding and teary eyed. She could taste the danger as she watched the big beat-up car slow down in front of the Majik Market across the street, the driver grimly pushing a barrel through the window. Then she panicked when there was a big bang and several people screamed and fell. Maybe she better go hide behind her mother. But she did not want her mother to see her scared half to death. With wobbly legs she heard screams and moans of agony, hoping she would not have to explain her brief absence. If Mommy found out she had been near the street, she might pull her hair or pinch her ears. She crept to the door and blasting music filled her ears. Great, her mother was preoccupied with the stereo.

Her mother was suddenly at the screen door looking at her.

"Angel, I didn't know you were out here," her mother said, feigning concern. "I've been looking all over the house for you."

"Really, Mommy?" she said surprisingly.

Still wobbly legged, she settled into a rotting rocking chair on the porch, as her mother, who was playing dumb, looked at her more carefully. Her mother cracked the screen door and stepped outside in the humid heat. She saw the gathering crowd at the store and heard the sirens. Lena heard her mother say that it must have been a drive by shooting over a drug deal gone bad.

"You look upset, Angel."

"Really," she said, playing the "dumb" game.

"So you are upset."

"Oh, no, Mommy," she played along.

"Angel, you're face is white as a ghost. Tell Mommy what's wrong," her mother said tenderly. "Come on, please."

Her mother stared, Lena ignored her, wondering if her lying was about to be revealed.

"I said, I'm not upset, Mommy." She stared at tiny yellow buds floating delicately down from two towering trees, then asked timidly. "Mommy, where's Dadee?"

Anger showed on her mother's face.

"You're being elusive," her mother complained, "and I don't know why." She went back inside, slamming the flimsy door behind her.

Police cars screeched to a stop at the Majik Market. Lena's fear was subsiding now. The black shape of a bird floated past then melted into glimmering heat. She felt at ease now that her mother had quit questioning her. She was sorry for lying, but told herself it was okay because she could not face her mother's hostility.

A half an hour later her mother returned with a changed look on her face. She was clad in a sheer T-shirt, braless, her shorts pulled deep into her crotch.

"Let's go, Angel," she happily said.

"To where, Mommy?"

"To the store. Mommy's goin' to buy you something better than a diamond ring."

"What's a diamond ring?" She was not afraid now. "Is it something to eat?"

"No, it's something you wear."

"Where, Mommy?"

"On your finger, dummy, see?" Her mother extended her

left hand, presenting a flecked diamond encased in a white gold band.

"What's better than a diamond ring?" she inquired, annoyed at having to ask so many questions.

"A Popsicle."

"Oh, wow," she paused and blinked. 'What's a dummy, Mommy?"

"I don't know," her mother said in an irritated manner. "You're too inquisitive."

Her mother held her hand as she crossed the street. The hot asphalt burned her bare feet, invoking in her a vague memory of some uncertain event.

After they got in the store, and her mother was not looking, she ran her hand gently across a vanishing scar that covered all of her chest. She felt she had to do this behind her mother's back, and somewhere in the back of her mind she felt that her deceptive action was only proper.

Chapter Three

She lolled restlessly upon a beanbag. Her mother, sat before a mirror in string panties and a glistening gold necklace, applied a pearly liquid to her face, brushed back her hair, and smiled sweetly.

"Angel, Daddy won't be home till late tonight. You go to bed so you can get up when he gets in." Mother had a peculiar air about her that held Lena in suspense. "You be a good girl and Mommy'll buy you another Popsicle tomorrow, okay?"

"Awright," she sniffled, annoyed at her mother for sending her to bed so early.

"I'll wake you when Daddy comes home."

Something was wrong and Lena knew it. Her mother had always let her stay awake until the wee hours of the morning.

"You listen to Mommy," her mother raved, "and you'll grow up to be a smart girl. You'll give orders instead of taking them."

"Mommy. Mom...," she stopped in mid word, bridling a load of curiosity.

"What, Angel?"

"Never mind," she said, yawning.

"You're already tired. So get to bed," her mother ordered, kissing her mouth and smacking her behind playfully.

EYES OF A CHILD 27

She rose from the beanbag, unsure of why her mother's gaze was following her, and she felt uneasy as she went to her bedroom. Before entering the bedroom, she stopped, and was about to question her mother, then decided against it. Her mother always seemed to be scheming whenever her father was not present.

Although Lena was a preschooler, her maturity was closer to that of a third or fourth grader, her inquisitive personality was always searching for answers. As she flung herself upon the soft bed her innocent mind filled with deep anger. Lena was indignant at the way her mother had used kindness, smiles and sweetness just to send her away. Why does she have to act that way? she asked herself. Did she have something to hide? Lena was afraid she would have her hair yanked if her mother knew she was really angry.

It was much too early to go to sleep, but as the miserable moments dragged on, her eyes grew heavy as she gazed out from her bedroom window to a chocolate sky. One by one she counted the speckled stars until she drifted to a light sleep. Ding...Ding...Ding...Ding...The ticktock clock sang.

Ding...Ding...Ding. Lena awakened fully by the twelfth metallic chime. The house was dark and chilly. Where was Mother? Had Daddy come home? A car hummed past, illuminating the house with a flash of headlights, then vanished, leaving her again in gloomy darkness. A quiet creaking resounded through the house. The night was spooky and she curled into a fetal position, longing to snuggle up against her parents. As though for safety, she hugged her filth encrusted bunny rabbit when she saw the glowing red eyes of a hungry rat dart underneath the dresser. Stricken with near panic, she longed for the safety of her parents. She imagined the rat climbing atop the bed and biting her on the neck.

"Mommy," she whispered in a pleading tone as she heard the rat scratching at the walls.

She was scared; she wanted her mother.

"Mommy," she whispered as loud as she dared.

Nothing. Had Mommy left her all alone? She stared at the dresser where the rat had run, then at the narrow doorway, which seemed to be slowly closing, and she noticed a faint movement in the house. Was a vampire walking in the house? She got out of bed hugging her bunny rabbit to her chest, and tiptoed in a crouch toward her mother's bedroom and the movement had suddenly mysteriously vanished. She was certain the vampire had seen her and was about to spring out of the dark and pounce on her. She had better find her Mommy, quick. If vampires were not real they would not show them on the horror movies her mother always watched.

"Mommy?" she whispered as she trembled, looking, knowing that a vampire was walking in the house.

A strange feeling told her to keep quiet. She passed the cluttered bathroom, which was adjacent to her mother's bedroom, from which emitted a deep silence; the doorway was filled with a scary but lesser darkness that gave her enough courage to move ahead. Her legs trembled and she was too scared to cry. As darkness poured from the doorway she tiptoed slowly and cautiously into the bedroom. Her eyes adjusted and, instead of a vampire, she noticed on the floor the faint image of her nude mother on hands and knees, whimpering, rocking back and forth. Confused, she could not stop staring.

Why was her mother crying? Was she praying? Her absorbing eyes saw that she was not alone, but with a big bad man. He was awkwardly attached to her mother from behind. What was he doing to her mother? Who was he? Was he hurting her mother? And why was she matching his thrusts? These disturbing questions puzzled her still more. Shocked at what was happening, she seemed frozen in place, crushing the bunny to her chest. A sharper adjustment of her eyes in the darkness of the room revealed a shiny oil on her mother's shapely buttocks, as the man pumped heartily. She would have intervened, but her shocked body felt like a stump of lead.

The pumping of the man became quite desperate, so urgent he sounded like a man who had sprinted a marathon, and then he suddenly came to a dead stop as he hunched over her back. Mommy had stopped whimpering, but the bad man was still massaging her glistening buttocks. She finally eased her grip on the Easter bunny, then her leaden body quickly began shedding its heavy burden. She was so happy that that man had stopped hurting her mother. Then she heard slippery body movement and her mother turning her way.

"Angel?" her mother said so sweetly.

"Shhhhh," the bad man said.

Lena stiffened again when the naked, muscular man rose from his knees. She assumed that the long, fuzzy thing dangling between his legs was a cat's tail put on backwards.

"Lena, come here!" There was such sweetness in her mother's words that it made Lena think that maybe her mother really did love her.

She squeezed her bunny rabbit tight.

"Why were you watchin' me?" her mother inquired penitently.

She stayed silent because she was unable to keep her eyes off the man.

"You waitin' for Daddy?" her mother asked with more sweet words

"Nooo...no," she whined.

"That little snot mine, Crystal?" the man asked, but with a relieved tone.

"Could be," her mother said to him.

A sad, pitiful thought of her father, angry and drawn, bloomed in her consciousness and she realized that this strange, bad man had violated her father's household.

"Why aren't you sleepin', Lena?" Her mother's tone was tender, extremely sweet now.

While she remained quiet, her mother straightened her back and pushed out her bulging breasts.

"She's staring at it," the man said. "Takin' after you, Crystal."

Lena's mother affirmed the fact with an anxious, muffled groan.

Lena wanted to hide, but held back. Had she angered her mother? Would Mother yank her hair again? But she was not the blame; she had been awakened by the ticktock clock.

"Why were you watchin' me?" her mother inquired again, still in an extremely sweet tone.

"I don't know," she crackled. "A rat in my room, Mommy."

Her chunky mother was slipping into her panties and Lena sensed a coconut aroma that made her think of candy and she got hungry and almost forgot her plight. In her mind she imagined her father crashing through the front door.

"Mommy?" She wanted to tell her mother she thought a blood sucking vampire was in the house and she was scared.

"Go to your room. I'll be with you in a minute," her mother said.

"Awright," she obeyed.

She crept through the dark, into her bedroom, and sat on the edge of the bed, lifting her tiny feet so the rat would not bite her toes. She had unveiled the private life that her mother led outside her father's and now she felt a distrust she had never felt before. Another passing car flashed a gleam of light into the room through the shabby Cookie Monster curtains. Despite her sweet words, she sensed a potential violence in her relationship with her mother, and when she tried to understand why she got confused. Movement in the house alerted her senses. She lifted her chin when she thought the man had slipped out of the house as silently as he had slipped in. The door scraped shut. She heard her mother bolt the door. How would her mother ever regain her trust? Warily she looked for the rat on the dresser; she folded her arms around her bunny rabbit and felt secure by the fuzzy slick fur. Her mother, naked and giggling, slipped into the bedroom. She approached Lena with open arms and a bad heart.

"I thought you were sleepin', Angel," she said, embracing Lena tenderly to her bare breasts. "I was surprised you were watchin' me. But that's okay."

"I'm sorry, Mommy." When her breasts touched her face it made Lena remember when she was a little girl how she used to sleep between Mommy's legs and used her center as a pillow. "But I needed you."

"I was busy, as you could see, Angel. But why were you just standing there staring?"

"I was scared," she said, feeling ashamed of being scared at her age.

"How come you were scared?"

"Because you were crying," she said in a timid tone.

She had imposed on her mother's hidden life. Distrust urged her to play dumb. Her mother had not yet moved to discuss what had happened and this soothed her.

"Sometimes you cry when you're happy," her mother told her bluntly.

She could easily sense that her mother was not ashamed of the event and obviously felt she did not owe Lena an explanation. She was normal now, perfectly normal. Lena was baffled. Her mother was as nasty as a cockroach. "You do...?"

"Uh, huh."

"Ohhh," she mumbled.

"Understand, Angel?" her mother asked.

Lena was uncomfortable with the answers her mother gave and was suddenly gripped with a strange fear that made her want to crawl underneath the bed and hide until the feeling of shock wore off, but her knees felt like they had ossified.

"Why are you so quiet?" her mother asked.

"The man, Mommy..."

Her voice died away as her mother's face seemed to wither, contorted like the face of a witch.

"Don't worry about that man."

"Awright, Mommy."

"Now, Lena, forget about the whole episode, okay? That man is Mommy's friend."

"Awright," she whispered hesitantly, afraid that the man might return and make her mother cry again.

Although fear had seemed to overwhelm her, she did respect her mother's boldness to speak with such naked truth. She was sure that she was being taught a highly momentous lesson.

"And about what happened tonight is strictly Mommy's business, so let's just keep it a secret between the two of us for Daddy's sake, okay, Angel?"

"Awright," she agreed.

Her mother gingerly kissed her on the face.

"Mommy, why was that man leaning over you? Why was he jerking like that? It looked like he was trying to shake your brains out. And why was he hurting you?"

Her mother's face dimmed, then brightened, and she stood upright, pushed out her breasts, raked her hands through her hair, and unleashed a silly giggle which resembled an ignorant person, or a person who lived in a world of all her own.

"Hurtin' me? No, Angel, it only looked that way..." She licked her lips, mumbling: "He was pleasuring me. It felt so good. He can shake my brains out anytime he wants. Some day you'll understand."

"I will?"

Her mother was acutely emphatic. "Angel, you sure will,

EYES OF A CHILD 33

Mommy'll see to it."

"Awright," she sighed, watching as her mother cupped and rubbed her sagging breasts for a moment as if they were sore. What a sly, treacherous mother she had!

"And Daddy'll be proud, too."

"He will?"

"Yes, Angel."

The thought of her mother kneeling for that strange man was rapidly vanishing.

"Mommy," she said, trying to smile.

"Yes, Angel?"

"My Popsicle. You said you'd buy me one tomorrow."

Milky moonlight suddenly poured into the room, making her mother's nakedness more visible.

"It's not tomorrow yet," her mother explained. She stopped squeezing her breast. "Daddy should be home soon. Don't forget; let's keep it a secret, okay?"

"Awright, Mommy."

"Okay, go back to bed till Daddy comes."

With keen eyes, she watched her half-naked mother walk from the bedroom. She could not wait to get her Popsicle, and from now on she would be the center of her mother's attention. What exalted her confidence was that her mother was teaching her the lessons of deception. She was unsure of the importance of that deception, but she was certain that her mother was preparing her for the journey into life's dilemmas. She did not like being a liar but if that was what her mother wanted then she had no choice. She had never seen such a liar, and hoped if she became a liar, that someday she could be just as skillful as her mother. Surprisingly that frightful episode with that pumping man was quickly fading by her anticipation to awaken in the morning and get her Popsicle.

After that night, strange men wearing cat tails lurked in her dreams.

Chapter Four

Early one Saturday morning Lena crept in her father's bedroom. She was pleased to see him sleeping and not in dispute with her mother. She climbed on the bed, careful not to awaken him, straddled his stomach, and then began jumping up and down, squealing loudly in delight as she attempted to wake him. She laughed, pushing on his inert form, pulling on his hair, wondering why he had not yet responded to her affection.

"Lena," her mother called to her. "Shhhhh, I'm trying to sleep."

"Shhhhh?" Lena taunted her mother slyly, putting a little finger to her lips.

Ignoring her mother, she lowered her face to her father's then bit at his nose. Her father opened his eyes, pretended not to notice her, then unleashed a playful growl and sat up in bed.

"What are you trying to do?" her father affected disapproval.

"A bite, Dadee." Lena bared her brown teeth, then snapped again at her father's nose. She loved to please him. She growled, exposed her bottom row of teeth, holding a vampiric look until her mother cut in.

"A big baby and a small baby." Crystal smiled.

Lena was satisfied. Just like she had predicted, her mother would favor her as well as her daddy.

And Lena did not care, even if she had accidentally compelled her mother to do so.

Lena could see that her father's eyes were filled with bewilderment at her mother's merry mood.

"Who's the big baby, Crystal?" her father asked teasingly.

"I'll have to think about it," Crystal countered, smiling.

While her father's face was averted Lena lunged forward, trying to bite his nose.

"Enough of that, little lady," her father said gleefully. "Ask Mommy if we can go to the zoo today."

"Mommy?" Lena practically yelled.

"Yes, Angel," Crystal interrupted.

"Good," her father said. "Go and get ready."

"Awright," Lena obeyed.

She clambered from the bed and trotted for the bathroom where she proceeded to wash her hands and face with scented soap. When she finished she could hear her parents laughing. After drying, she headed for her room and got dressed, thinking of the zoo, then hurried back into their company.

"Lena," her father said.

"What?" she questioned.

Her father eyed her closely. "That was fast."

"I know," she said happily.

"That's the fastest you've ever got ready," he said and moved to dress.

Already she could smell the buttered popcorn and hear the monkeys screeching. Anxiously, she paced about the bedroom, terribly excited, wishing her parents would hurry. She did not want to rush them, so she waited out on the porch. Why was she always so anxious?

Lena had seen only two cars whiz past the house by the

time her mother and father appeared. They Piled in the car and blended in with straying traffic. Meanwhile, her heart raced frantically as they sped west on I-595 to Markham Park Zoo. The grounds reeked of animal dung; the looming sun heated the day without mercy; dandelion puffs floated in the sky like white sheer.

Lena broke away from her parents and hurried to a cage of wild dogs that were moaning viciously, their pink tongues dripping saliva.

"Don't lean on the fence," her father said nervously, motioning at the loudest dog that was taking interest in her.

"Dadee," Lena whined with a smile. "I wanna pet 'im."

"No, no, no," her father scolded. "Those dogs are wild; they'll eat you up." He pointed at a sign on the cage with fluorescent red letters, which read: Dangerous dogs.

"You see that sign?" her father emphasized. "Tell me what it says?"

"Dan-dangerous d-dogs," Lena stammered.

"Now do you want those dogs to rip you to pieces?" her father growled.

"No," Lena shouted defensively. "They'd be picking up pieces of me a year from now."

"Then stay away from the fence," her father ordered.

"Awright," Lena shouted again.

With the echoes of the howling dogs still in her ears Lena caught sight of some of the bad, neighborhood kids coming her way. She sensed they would harass her as they did a hundred times before. She remembered what her father had said about dope's doing dope so she refused to associate with those slum kids. They were unfortunate victims of the neighborhood slum, but they were the white trash of the bunch, her father had explained on so many occasions she had it memorized. The others were just winos and derelicts and thieves, nothing to be scoffed at. But there was probably no hope for any of them.

When they neared she waved politely, hoping to ward off any insults.

One of the kids made a mocking face at her and another stuck out her tongue and, to make things worse, she had a handful of popcorn thrown in her direction, and a rotten apple whizzed over her head. They were not only trash but were kind of violent too. She ignored them, but she felt sad. They were harassing her for hanging with her parents, for living in the filthiest of the dilapidated shacks in the drug infested neighborhood, of the joke that her father, Jim Smith, a former college professor who worked the night shift at the Seven Eleven for pennies and fought with the drunks. She wished she could walk the streets like them and pick on other kids even though it was wrong. But they were dope's who did dope and there was no hope for those slimy slum bums, who made her feel sad and as cheap as a penny.

"Lena," her father reminded, "that's white trash."

"I know, Dadee," Lena wailed in a hurt tone.

She walked on, attracted to a cage of hurtling monkeys. She screamed in glee when a baby monkey swung from a bar, did a somersault in midair and latched on to its mother's back. The monkeys screeched and screamed and put out their hands for peanuts and bananas.

They walked toward the food stands, which had popcorn, hotdogs, hamburgers, sausages, sodas, candy apples, balloons, and blue, pink and yellow puffs of cotton candy. After a rest and a drink, Lena and her parents walked past idling crowds, passing lazy lions, chimpanzees, orangutans and a grunting hog weaning its frisky babies. They enjoyed the billy goats, horses, listless possums, raucous raccoons, pheasants and scores of rare wildlife.

They looked over a wall at a pit of slithering snakes basking in the midday heat.

"Let's go see the birds," Lena said.

"You don't like snakes?" her father asked, laughing.

"She's scared," her mother taunted.

"Huh, uh," Lena protested. The sneakiness of the snakes reminded her of her mother and she did not want her day ruined. "I wanna see the parrot birds."

On their way to the parrot jungle they passed reindeer, bears, and idling peacocks attracting attention.

"There are the parrot birds," Lena said with bubbling glee.

"You're right," her father agreed.

"Can I feed the birdies?" Lena asked, holding tightly onto her bag of freshly popped popcorn.

"No," her mother cut in. "They might bite you."

"You can feed the birds," her father overrode her mother. "Parrots don't bite."

"Awright, Dadee," Lena said and fell silent.

A steady drone of birdcalls echoed in the air. They walked under swaying pine trees and over a wooden bridge under which gurgled a silver stream.

They entered a clearing in the thicket where a crowd of people was tightly jammed together. A big red bird with green splashes, quietly poised itself on the shoulder of a man, dressed in a black silky suit.

"He's forty years old ," the man said. "He's from the jungles of Brazil, and will live to be one hundred and two years old."

The man pulled a peanut from his pocket and flipped it in the air. The audience cheered when the bird snatched and swallowed it in one lightning move. When the man snapped his fingers, the bird alighted at once onto his extended arm. An excited murmur came from the audience.

"Can we get closer, Dadee?" Lena said, fascinated.

"Sure," her father said.

They walked around the crowd to the front. Lena saw

her mother lagging behind. When the bird was returned to its cage a furious fluttering of feathers could be seen and a shrill squawk rang out twice. All the other birds joined in and whistled, chirped, and sang out into the hot afternoon.

The man returned with a long yellow bird with a fuzzy white cap listlessly perched on his head. The audience applauded loudly. Lena watched excitedly at the foot of the crowd. The man clapped his hands and the listless look left the bird. Another clap and the bird fluttered down to the man's feet. From his pocket, he pulled out a peanut and held it above the bird. The bird squawked but did not move. He let the peanut fall and the bird swallowed it before it touched the ground. A contented roar came from the audience.

"Are those parrot birds, Dadee?" Lena asked.

"I think so," her father said.

"Can I feed 'em?" She held up her popcorn.

"No, I don't think you're allowed," her father apologized.

Amazed, Lena screamed and cheered at every different bird. Afterwards, they walked away and stumbled upon a quiet, sad looking gorilla. How sad, Lena thought. A bumblebee hummed past. Then a dragonfly. The heat was fading. The gorilla kept its eyes on Lena's popcorn and, when her parents were not watching, she stuck the bag of popcorn through the bars and the gorilla snatched it from her grip.

Lena stumbled back and let out a shrill scream that startled her parents.

"That damn beast could have ripped off your arm,' her father yelled.

"That thing is harmless," her mother insisted.

"Shut up," her father shouted, then turned to Lena. "Don't trust anything. You hear me?"

"Yeah," Lena answered.

"I've seen enough," her mother said, "let's go."

The gorilla wagged its head, gobbled the popcorn, then the bag.

Lena had a dazed look on her face. She moved toward her parents when the gorilla suddenly beat on its chest and bared huge thick teeth in a heinous way. She had never seen an animal so bold, but that boldness had a vague pity in it, for it seemed to know that it was forever locked in the cage.

A soothing laugh erupted from her father.

"Relax; you're safe; he can't get out," her father said. His voice still sounded shaky. "Just don't get too close, okay?"

"Awright," Lena complied.

"Let's go," her mother said again.

Still filled with anxiety, Lena's mind wandered, touching on everything but her mother's request. She was saddened at the thought of leaving the zoo. Some vague intuition told her that she would never again return to this luscious green heaven, where squirrels abounded happily, eating acorns and popcorn, where baby raccoons obediently followed parent raccoons, where lions silently lazed in the cloying heat, where piglets lolled freely underneath the drizzling rain, and where life in general seemed to fall properly in place. Gee, she thought, why can't I stay here forever?

Her mother's voice pulled her from her daydream: "Angel, let's go."

"Come on, Lena," her father said.

"Awright."

She lagged behind her parents. They walked for several minutes before reaching the exit.

"I was scared of that gorilla," Lena admitted.

"So was I," her father also admitted.

"He's harmless," her mother stressed in a tone of opposition. "I've never seen such babies."

Lena trailed after her parents, then thought of herself with only one arm. A nervous, dejected feeling engulfed her as she left with a sad heart.

Chapter Five

"I bet," Lena's father said loudly as he came home from work in a melancholy mood, "that someone has been mistreating my Lena."

Lena rose from the dirty floor, extending her arms to her father.

"Uh, huh, Dadee."

Her father took her in his arms, stroked her hair, appearing deeply troubled. Her mother glared with guilty eyes, sipping on her coffee.

"Jim, Lena's my concern too," she said.

"Dadee, what's wrong?" Lena asked. "What are you and Mommy arguing about?"

"Abuse. Child abuse," her father said angrily.

"What's that?" Lena questioned.

"You don't know?" her father sounded surprised.

"No, Dadee, I don't."

"Well, you've experienced it, even if you don't know what it means," her father said.

"You and Mommy goin' to fight?" she crackled, hoping for an answer from either of her parents.

"I don't know, but we gotta talk," her father said. "I'm sick and tired of wondering about things. Nobody's gonna bother you if I can help it. So, go to your room and play and

Daddy'll be with you later."

"Awright, Dadee." She smiled with joy at all the attention; her father lowered her to the floor. She had noticed that her father's voice had slowly risen to a grim monotone and it sounded like she was learning some important lesson. Gleefully, she disappeared from the living room.

Lena sensed that something terrible was taking shape between her parents, that a showdown between them was coming, and her nervousness suddenly intensified her fearful feeling of uncertainty. It was all her fault. But why? She noticed a long silence then a heated argument abruptly erupted between her mother and father.

"What now, Jim?" Her mother spoke meanly. "Ain't I takin' good enough care of our daughter?"

"I just wanna know the truth of what's goin' on!" her father yelled viciously.

Her mother threw down her coffee, her temper flaring.

"Jim, you can see what's going on! I'm takin' care of Lena, and doing a damn good job!"

"I don't believe you!" her father countered in a frenzy.

"I don't care what you believe!" her mother shouted defiantly. "My mother even said I was doing a good job."

"You're a damn child abuser just like your mother," her father said bluntly. "You sure are."

"You know nothing. All you ever do is condemn. My mother. My mother. Leave my mother alone."

"How can I when she put your dog to sleep when you moved in with me. You don t have to be a child abuser too. I'll help you not to be a child abuser. You got to stop being a child abuser someday, Crystal."

Oh, no! Lena had not wanted her parents fighting like that. She noticed her face turn white and tight. She peered around the threshold and saw her father standing close to her mother, and shouting. "I'll take Lena away and you'll never see her again. So you better stop mistreating her."

"Me, mistreating Lena?" she squealed, trying to sound innocent. "My own flesh'n blood?"

"That's right!" her father insisted, his lips contorted in anger. "And don't try'n deny it."

"Don't put words in my mouth!" her mother screamed.

"I'll call the authorities!" her father hollered.

"You're not that stupid!" her mother shouted. "You only pretend to be that stupid."

"How is that being stupid?" her father asked, quieting, a concerned look on his face.

"I'll say you molested her," her mother said. "They'll take her away from both of us."

"Away from you," her father corrected. "You're unfit. You probably would say I molested her."

Lena was shaking. She felt unsafe, intimidated. The awareness settled on her that her mother was trying to shift unearned blame to her father. Lena was shocked. The thought of being taken away from her parents made her more afraid. Lena withdrew back into the bedroom as the argument diminished and sat before a dismantled wooden puzzle. Suddenly, a longing to be close to her parents filled her. Big salty tears fell from her eyes. She leaned her head on the puzzle pieces and whimpered silently. At length, her crying stopped and she stretched out on the filthy carpet.

"She's playing us against one another," she heard her mother say.

"It's you, Crystal, not her," her father corrected.

"It is?"

"Yes it is." Her father's voice started to rise.

"You wanna argue some more?" her mother whispered nastily.

"We'll finish this later," her father promised.

Lena whined, rolled on her side and looked at her parents, not caring to hide her tears. She stood, trembling, and reached out her arms, walking toward her father, wanting to be held.

"I'm sick, Dadee," Lena cried.

"You'll be okay," her father said.

"Okay, girl. It's time for bed," her mother said.

Father turned out the light. While in the dark, Lena was overcome by a feeling of a dreamy life, an unreal, abstract life, suspended in meaninglessness, a feared life. A strong arm lifted her off the floor.

"Stop crying," her father pleaded worriedly.

"Awright," Lena said, crying louder, squeezing her father's neck.

"She's feelin' sorry for herself," her mother interrupted.

She could see her father eye her mother evilly. They were facing each other like two soldiers waiting for the other to drop his guard. Both wanted to win and both were too stubborn to go down in defeat. A sudden rumble shattered the darkness and she practically froze.

"Relax," father whispered, "it's only thunder."

The windows slightly rattled from a strong breeze and she looked out in the night and she could see trees swaying and branches trembling like her. Further down the road, the headlights of passing cars looked like blurred eyes of hope in a hopeless night. A flash of lighting lit up the darkness and she squeezed her father's neck tighter when thunder rumbled like death.

"It's probably going to rain," her mother added.

Lena knew that her refuge was with her father.

She felt that her mother was envious when they were together.

When they reentered the living room and stood in the dark, the sound of falling rain hummed and drummed the rooftop. Flickering television light made the features of her mother's face contort and turned her upright posture to a gruesome hunch.

"I don't wanna go to sleep," Lena whined. "I want to stay with you, Dadee."

"Daddy can't hold you all night, Angel," her mother sounded indignant.

"I'll sit with her for a while," her father said.

Her mother stood awkwardly, looking at Lena with an unpleasant smile while switching off the television. "Okay, just for a little while," she said.

"Maybe I shouldn't have yelled so loud." Her father sounded regretful.

"It didn't hurt her," she said.

"Like hell it didn't," he mumbled. "She's scared half to death."

"That's just part of growing up," her mother said. "What you oughta do is stop making false accusations toward me."

"I'm not making false accusations," her father emphasized.

"You sure in hell are," her mother defended.

They finally quieted, and her father looked away from her defensive mother. Lena eased her arms from around her father's neck. Mother moaned and left the living room. Lena was agitated with the fact that her mother had had the last word with her father. She glanced over her father's shoulder at mother's figure moving away in the gloom. A feeling of triumph replaced the fear as she was now alone with her father. She turned to him.

"Dadee, don't leave me, I'm scared," Lena whispered.

"I won't let no one ever bother you again," her father said with a forced smile.

"Awright," she mumbled.

She fell asleep in her father's arms in the living room until she was awakened by morning sunlight splashing through the screen door onto her tiny Anglo face.

"You think Mommy is mad?" Lena asked, rubbing her eyes with her tiny fists.

"It doesn't matter if she is," her father said harshly.

"I don't wanna be left all alone," Lena breathed.

"You won't be," her father promised.

Chapter Six

Since she was one year old Lena continuously had the sniffles and other childhood ailments, most of the time accompanied with a fever as high as 105 degrees. Her father said that it was from run down living conditions. Her mother disagreed and said that it was from low resistance and all children her age were stricken with colds, flues, fevers, viruses, and that was the norm for a child of four. Early one morning, as she was playing with her toys, a growing nausea churned strangely in the pit of her stomach, and she felt like vomiting. She walked weakly to her mother and asked for some soda. She grabbed Lena angrily by the hair, scolding her for disturbing her while she was busy. Shaking, she hurried away from Mommy, because Mommy was mad, ignoring her aching skin turning unusually cold and clammy.

Then the dilapidated house, filled with thick, fresh cigarette smoke, produced a horrible reeking that began to get her sicker. She sat down upon the floor, doubled over to retch, afraid she was about to vomit her guts out all over her toys. Her mother kept puffing cigarettes while she watched her horror movies, blowing clouds of smoke above the TV, and then at Lena and straying flies during commercial breaks. Strange ugly faces in a dark, gloomy mist loomed deep in her mind, as her mother stormed into her bedroom with a cigarette stuck in her mouth.

"Angel, what's your problem, disturbing Mommy while I'm watching my movies."

"I'm sorry, Mommy," she mumbled quietly.

She tried to fight off the nausea but she found it was futile and she started to retch. Her thoughts had settled upon the face of her mother and she formed an image that she had grown thick fangs, was plotting to eat her and her long drooling tongue was licking her lips. Drawing her legs together, she doubled up in a fetal position, hoping the terror would soon be over.

"Don't eat me, Mommy," she begged pitifully.

A moment of silence blanketed her, slightly easing her fear. She saw the darkness in her mind get bright, and she saw her mother's fangs grow bigger and bigger, almost reaching her. Her mother hissed and groaned and bared a row of razor sharp teeth that seemed anxious to bite. As her stomach ached, she thought that she was going to die, and she needed help. She finally opened her eyes and she saw her mother kneeling beside her.

"Angel, you feelin' okay?"

Her mother's face was so distorted that she closed her eyes immediately, hoping she was dreaming, shivering and nauseated with stomach pain that felt like a burning block of rock.

"Don't eat me. I don't wanna be eaten," she whispered.

Her mother groaned and puffed on her cigarette.

"Always lookin' for attention," her mother said, stroking Lena's damp curls.

Pain kept burning hotly inside her stomach, and her feeble resistance made her feel so ill that she groaned pathetically.

"What's wrong, Lena?" her mother rudely asked, growing angry that her daughter wanted all the attention.

She doubled up tighter, squeezing her arms to her body to resist the cold. The anger in her mother's voice escalated.

"Lena, now what's wrong?" her mother demanded.

She did not answer. She was so sick. Her mother shook her and saw sweat on her face as she lay on the floor, shaking like a leaf. Her mother started to wonder.

"You don't seem to want to listen to your mother," her mother said.

She struggled grimly to answer, to muster enough strength to overcome her misery.

"You're acting stranger today, Angel!" her mother said with a sudden concern in her voice. "Stranger than a week ago."

She pulled at Lena's almost lifeless form. Shivers forced her small, decayed teeth to chatter.

"Something's wrong with you, Angel," her mother mumbled, finally, fearfully.

Lena groaned her agreement. Body discomfort left her so miserable she refused to utter another word. Weakness suffused her; sleep prevailed. When she awoke she was in her father's car. He was driving her to the hospital. There were people dressed in white carrying her into the emergency room; needles pricking her thighs; her father at her bedside; her mother's face holding a sly grin; being diagnosed with infectious hepatitis A. She awoke from a deep sleep to find herself strapped to a bed with an intravenous needle taped to her wrist. Seeing herself in this helpless position, she abruptly started trembling in fear. Her eyes darted about for her father, but he was nowhere to be seen. If only she could find her father she would be safe. She tried to free herself but was too weak.

"Dadee," she cried in fear.

Again she failed to free herself. She had shaken the needle slightly loose and it now hurt her.

"Dadee, help!" she yelled, terrified that she may be forever strapped to the bed.

At last she freed her left arm and desperately tried to unstrap the belts that secured her to the bed. This freedom coupling with the inability to free herself altogether only added to her fear. Lena was now certain that she had been taken away from her parents. A thousand other fears sifted through her mind.

"Help me!" she screamed. "Help me, Dadee!"

Fluorescent lights fluttered on and she recognized her father. Lena reached out frantically with her left arm, imploring security, releasing vivid images of imaginary beliefs. She relaxed a little when her father's tight, thin lips touched her cheek.

"Relax, honey," he said. "You'll be all right."

"Unstrap me, Dadee," she cried.

The doctor had entered and studied her condition.

"She's a long way from recovery," he said. "The yellowing has deepened and the fever has gone up."

"When will I be able to take her home?" her father asked.

"In a month I presume, as long as she starts eating," the doctor said. "Unstrap her till she relaxes a little more."

He unstrapped her and pacified her back to normalcy.

"Hold me, Dadee," she implored, extending her arms.

"I can't do that. You're too sick right now," he pampered her.

She fell that day into a hepatic hallucination, mouth gaping, eyes gazing off into another dimension, unaware of her surroundings, as limp as a Barbie doll. She was suddenly flooded with dread, for next to her hospital bed was a thick marble slab on which dead people were prepared for burial. Standing rigidly near the slab was a skeleton-faced undertaker whose rotting flesh stank of the pungent odor of formaldehyde that seemed to ooze from all his pores. Horrified, she saw the undertaker's head twist on its socket and saw his thin, wasted legs turning her way and his skeletal arms fumbling with a tool to drain her blood, feet scraping the floor, coming anxiously for her.

"I'm not dead," she groaned in horror.

Still he approached and his eyes, empty sockets of death, stared straight at her bulging jugulars.

"Please, don't drain my blood, I'll never see my daddy again," she cried, shielding her face with her pillow.

With a morbid groan the undertaker snatched the pillow from her face and she saw him leaning over her, about to carry her to the slab so he could insert the tool in her jugular vein and drain her blood to prepare her for burial....

"Don't! Don't!" she pleaded.

Then she abruptly fell into relief that he had somehow dissipated.

A while later she gazed warily about. Her father was not there. She sighed deeply, for she was not strapped in place. A beckoning force pulled her attention to the entrance of her room, where an ugly creature stood. Then she saw it was really her mother, holding a metal pot of boiling coffee, and coming right at her. Her eyes bulged in shock as her mother aimed at her and poised herself to throw the coffee on her, coffee so hot that it began to melt holes through the pot, sizzling as it hit the floor

"I'm gonna burn you, Lena," her mother said, her brow wrinkling angrily, hatefully. "Yeah, I'm gonna burn my little girl. Burn her so bad that her Daddy will feel the burn..."

"No don't!" she begged. "Please, don't, Mommy!"

She twisted onto her stomach and pressed her face into the sheets, wrapping her arms around her head, waiting for the coffee to burn her flesh off her bones. Then her father was there with her and she tried to jump into his arms, to get away from a monstrous mother whose contorted form suddenly vanished into thin air.

Her father's eyes were tired, troubled. With fumbling hands, her mother held a crystal vase with blooming roses. The aroma from the roses sparked a soothing feeling in Lena, which made her want to hold them.

"Hi, Angel," her mother said, acting as though Lena had never been sick. "How are you?"

"I don't feel too good," Lena whined pitifully. "I'm wet too."

Without uttering a word, her father lowered the side railing to the hospital bed. She sat up and smiled sickly, looking like she wanted to stand but did not have the energy. Her father knelt down and gently scooped her up into his arms.

"You are wet," her father mumbled. "Yellow too."

"I know," she wailed. "I wanna go home, Dadee."

"After the doctor sees you," her father hugged her. "Don't cry. You won't be here forever." He nodded as redheaded Dr. Jeff Ehrlich entered. "Hi, Jeff, good to see you."

"Likewise, Jim." He greeted Lena's mother then righted his thick eyeglasses as he turned to Lena and lifted her eyelids.

"The yellowing will last for about six more months, and the nausea will linger for a while but it will gradually leave altogether, and it's okay to take her home," Dr. Ehrlich said. "With time her appetite will return to normal. She's doing very well." He winked at Lena. "I see someone brought you roses, little lady."

Lena shook her head in thankful acknowledgment.

Dr. Ehrlich studied Lena's chart then he looked up. "Her blood tests show that her yellowing is a two point five," he explained. "Down from a seven point six two weeks ago. Just a slight inflammation of the liver is all she has now. When she was having the hallucinations, had her condition turned for the worse, and she had fallen into a hepatic coma, she probably would have died within ten days unless a miracle was performed. I would have been helpless to help her. But she's in no danger now and that's all in the past." Then with a big grin on his freckled face, he stared directly into Lena's unwavering eyes. "You'll have to lay off the booze for at least six months, little lady. Can you handle that?"

Even Lena erupted in laughter with everybody else, although she did not quite grasp the humor in it.

"Uh, huh, Dr. Ehrlich," she mumbled and everybody laughed again.

"Okay, Jim, I got other patients to see," Dr. Ehrlich confessed. "But I'll see you at Seven Eleven tonight. If you see Lisa, tell her I want to see her."

"Sure thing, Jeff."

For the moment Lena was totally drenched in security. She folded her arms and rested her head on her father's shoulder, grateful for Dr. Ehrlich's playful mood, but slightly worried he might keep her hospitalized.

She was happy to see him leave to check on other cute little kids and her appetite did begin to slowly return and within days she had regained much of her strength. Happily she devoured sodas, Slurpees, Hershey bars, Oreos, Blow Pops, Animal Crackers, cookies and Nabisco ice cream and welcomed an energetic surge sweeping through her which invigorated her enough to play with her toys on the porch and watch blackbirds feeding in the trees. She enjoyed playing in the dirt, throwing rocks, or stomping on bugs with her bare feet. Since she had almost recovered now, not only did her father cut off the junk food, but he stopped enticing her with visits to Burger King and McDonald's to bring home bags of juicy hamburgers and greasy fries to stimulate her appetite and clog her arteries.

"Take me for a hamburger, so I can get fat, flabby and ugly," she implored. "Please, Dadee."

"You're no longer sick," he said. "Only sick people get that service. You got to get back to three decent meals a day, so you can stay healthy, mentally wealthy, and sweet as honey, just like your Easter bunny."

She whined, cried, threw a tantrum, was envious of sick people, plotted to get her way.

But her father did not succumb to Lena's demands by going back to the night shift at the Seven Eleven while her mother attended to her needs. A day later a compulsive urge to do something to please her mother overtook her. She walked into forbidden ground and her mother lay naked in bed and sound asleep. Awake or not awake, she was determined to please her mother. Bursting with bubbling energy, she went back into the living room and began picking up papers that cluttered the floor. Her clothes fit pitifully on her petite, slender bones, though she had more weight now than before. On hands and knees, she crawled to every corner, to every tight spot of the room, and plucked up even the tiniest scraps of paper and lint. She neatly stacked a pile of her mother's dirty old shoes, which were concealed underneath an end table. Her knees were sore and she was about to rise when she noticed a piece of paper underneath the couch. She bent over and reached for it. It was slightly out of her reach.

Determined, she slipped between the couch and the floor, her nose inhaling fumes of decaying cloth. She now had it in her grip, but next to it was a hard object. With her curiosity mounting, her tiny fingers probed further and, no sooner had she gripped the paper and object, all in one fist, she felt cold metal crash upon her hand. Her fingers nearly broken, she could feel an agonizing streak of pain crawl up to her elbow and freeze. The pain jolted her, trapped her breath deep in her throat. Then she instantly heaved against a rising pillar of pain, unable to shake off enough pain to scream her head off. She felt like something held her in place, but she was actually stuck under the couch. Stimulated with her survival instinct, she struggled to free herself by the impossible task of lifting up the couch. She finally let out a scream so morbidly that her mother jumped from bed and ran to her aid without a second thought. She pulled herself free as swiftly as her mother had lifted up the couch, her right hand madly slapping at a rat trap, her morbid screams now more morbid.

Her mother freed her hand from the trap and it stemmed her flood of tears, though she kept whining and despairing, pitying herself, stricken with physical and mental hurt. She regarded her mother with sad eyes until her father hurried home from work, when she admitted she was hoping to please her mother when she had gotten her hand caught in the rat trap. She was again taken to the Hollywood Memorial Hospital where Dr. Ehrlich informed her parents that the injury had only fractured her baby finger. But had she succeeded in ripping away the rat trap, her finger may have come off with it.

Lena was deliberately open now in encouraging attention from her father, and he, filled with sympathy, approved of it despite her mother's objections.

Chapter Seven

One August day Lena stalked about her fenced in jungle-like backyard, banging with a baseball bat at knee-high grass, dry weeds, wildflowers, dragonflies, butterflies, and laboring honeybees. She was looking to smash in a rat's head like the way her mother had tried to step on her father's head one night, or to club a snake to death just for the fun of watching it hiss, slither and die. She saw a green lizard pulsing in the sun, smiled, advanced cat-like, raising the bat over her head, then swung, feeling proud as it whistled through the air and came down squarely upon the lizard's back. It bleeds yellow blood, she thought in delight. She stalked again, looking for another lizard to smash as a test to her accuracy. She froze, spotting a citrus fly idling above a limb of honeysuckle. She felt that smashing the fly would be more of a challenge than a defenseless lizard. With bat poised, she moved in for the kill. To her dismay it hummed off to a thick growth of poison ivy covering the fence. With renewed confidence, she stalked after it, but as she was ready to strike, the fly again hummed off, and this time, into the glare of the sun. She squinted her eyes and watched the black dot disappear. Wow. How could it fly directly into the sun when she could barely look into the sun? Well, she would ask her parents. Retracing her steps, she kept an eye out for something to smash and carried the baseball bat proudly over her shoulders.

"What are you doing?" the words echoed in her ears.

Great, her father was standing in the doorway in his jogging trunks.

"Playing," she said loudly. She advanced closer to her father and triumphantly revealed the bloodstain on her baseball bat. "I killed a lizar, Dadee. See the blood?"

"Yes, I see the blood," her father sounded mad.

"I killed 'im while he was taking a sunbath," she boasted to him.

"Why? Did he bite you?" her father questioned, wondering what prompted her to kill the lizard as he was scrutinizing the bloodstain.

"No." She smiled broadly. "He didn't get a chance."

"Who told you to kill lizards?"

"My Mommy told me to," Lena stiffly replied.

She had felt it wise to tell him the truth.

"Your Mommy told you to?" her father echoed, feigning disbelief. "Do you know that they eat all the bad bugs that live indoors?"

"They do?" Lena asked.

"They sure do," her father stressed. Then he let his eyes bulge to make her understand the seriousness of her act.

A fleeting compassion for the dead lizard swept through her.

"I sorry, Dadee."

"That's quite all right, but don't kill anymore lizards now." He wrinkled his brow in pretended grief. "Be a good girl."

"Awright."

Her father coaxed the bat from her grip, walked off, and sternly dumped it into a garbage can. Her father had expressed concern about a proper upbringing for her, and he turned to her now in a scolding fashion suited for a four year old.

"Never, never, kill lizards," he said strongly, as they stood beside a rainbowed flower hedge.

Her face lit up in agreement.

"As a matter of fact, it's a waste of time to even walk around with a baseball bat," her father complained. "Unless you plan on being a baseball player on an all male team, and I don't think you do."

"Awright," she whispered slightly puzzled.

"Let's find that lizard you killed." He took her gently by the arm.

"But it's dead!" Lena said nervously.

"Look," he continued to scold her. "You're not supposed to kill anything unless you're protecting yourself, especially a helpless lizard. You hear me. Lena?"

"Of course I hear you, Dadee," Lena said.

"If kids are taught to do bad things they think that it's okay to do bad things when they grow up," her father stressed.

She listened to her father, wondering if he was right.

"But I'm not bad," she sang in certainty.

"You're not following me," he said in a vexed tone. "Sometimes mother's unknowingly advise their kids wrongly, then when those kids grow up they think what they were advised of is right."

Her mind started to comprehend. In plain English she realized that her mother could be wrong without knowing it and, if her mother had been wrong even though thinking she was right, then it was definitely bad to kill lizards.

"Ohhh," Lena moaned.

"You understand?" her father asked, and he smiled tolerantly.

"I think so," Lena confessed.

"In time you'll understand everything," her father said, smiling and pulling Lena after him.

"To where, Dadee?" she asked, obediently following her father.

He took a few more steps with her then stopped.

"To the lizard," her father urged.

Lena did not want to find the lizard, because she was now filled with guilt. How bad it was to kill a playful lizard, how bad it was for mothers to be wrong, how bad it was for fathers to correct mothers who were not right, how bad it was for mothers to act out of spite and bask in bad delight at their children's plight. As her father searched for the dead lizard, her eyes kept darting to where it was. She slowed her pace, imagining a frenzied lizard bloating to the size of a dog and hungry for revenge.

"What's wrong?" her father asked.

"Nothing," she lied.

He stopped looking for the lizard, and glared at her for a couple of moments.

"Where's that poor dead lizard, Lena?" he finally asked.

"Somewhere," she answered quietly.

"Take me to it?" he prodded her.

"Awright," she agreed.

He followed as she led him to the dead lizard. Fire ants had swarmed over it, forming a red mound.

"Even a lizard deserves a proper burial, Lena," he said, gashing up damp soil with his bedroom slipper. "Pick him up and drop him in the hole."

"Huh?" she asked, shocked.

"You heard what I said," he answered politely, but firmly.

She stooped over and grabbed the lizard by its tail, but the tail broke off. She dropped the wiggling tail and jumped back. The ants scattered but some got on her fingers and she brushed them off.

"It's not dead, Dadee," she argued.

"It's dead," he assured. "Nerves in its tail make it wiggle."

Whining, she picked up the lifeless body, her fingers trembling, then quickly dropped it in the hole. She would never kill lizards again, for now she knew it was bad, and Mommy had been bad to tell her it was right, even if she believed she was right.

"Will you ever kill another lizard?" her father asked.

"No. That's bad," she replied with pity in her voice.

"I'll take that as a promise," he said, pleased.

"Awright," she answered.

"What if Mommy tells you that killing lizards is not wrong?" he prodded. "What will you say?"

"That's bad," she said with a stomp of her foot.

"You promise?"

"I sure do."

"I'll hold you to your promises."

He acted happy as he carried her back into the house. The ebbing of her fear suddenly brought the thought of the citrus fly back to her mind, how it could fly close to the sun? Maybe the smaller something was the closer it could safely get to the sun.

"Dadee, why can a fly fly into the sun?"

"What?" her father asked, looking surprised, but smiling.

"I seen a fly go into the sun," Lena explained, "but when I watched it going the sun hurt my eyes."

"That fly didn't fly into the sun," her father corrected. "It flew somewhere else. The sun's bright, that's why it hurt your eyes. Don't ever look directly up into the sun again, okay?"

"Awright." She fully understood.

After all her fear had fled, she seethed with defiance, but she could not understand why she felt defiant.

Chapter Eight

Kindergarten. The kids were running wild. The playroom was a scene of chaos. Toys were scattered everywhere. Shouts, whines, screams echoed off the walls. A bully kid, with a barrel for a stomach and a bulldog face, had taken another kids peanut butter cookies and started devouring them, stuffing the last one into his mouth before the other kid could say, "I'll tell my Mommy on you," or, "you're a bad boy and the teacher's gonna whip you," or better yet, "I hope you choke on the last crumb or swallow your tongue." Instead, the darkhaired, green eyed doll leaped up and bit him on the face and shrieked in glee when the bully gasped deeply, almost choked on the cookies, and let out a scream so loud that staff members intervened.

"Anthony, don't eat all her cookies before she bites you again," big, fat, black, grinning, Miss Debbie yelled.

"It's too late!" Anthony explained as he cried, chewed cookies and saliva, looking like dog gravy, spilled down his chin.

"That'll teach you, Anthony," Mr. Anderson taunted, shaking a finger at the naughty boy.

Lena watched the action in hilarity. She caught a glimpse of Mr. Anderson, the provost who was a tall, wiry, feminine man who had been talking to her father. He suddenly walked over to Anthony to inspect the teeth marks on his cheek. Merrily, Lena smiled in amazement. She saw Mr. Anderson scold Anthony and put him in a corner to be disciplined. Her father stood quietly, also taking in the bedlam. Maybe she would not be liked and would be made to stand in a corner and stare at two gray walls, she thought. She gloated at the entertainment, enjoyed it like she was at a circus, but wanted no part of it. Her eyes concentrated on her father's gestures while he spoke to Mr. Anderson. Lena snuggled against her father and wrapped her arm around his pants leg, as she watched Mr. Anderson offering him an enrollment form.

She did not like the school, or the stern looking Mr. Anderson, and Miss Debbie, looking like a sack of sausages that might burst at any moment, could be a side show at the circus. She wondered how her father found this school and, her heart sank when he accepted the white sheet.

"She'll be five in May," her father said.

"Good. I'll see you then."

They shook hands and departed.

Her father unlocked the car door and Lena climbed inside. She took another disgusted look at the ramshackle kindergarten building as her father drove away. She hoped to never return.

"That place looks like home," she said.

Lena was annoyed to find that her father was deliberately ignoring her.

"Dadee, is something wrong?"

Moodily, her father stared grimly ahead as the car rumbled when they changed lanes.

"Dadee?"

"It's time to mix with kids your own age and learn."

She leaned her face on her father's arm, intending to manipulate him, but he shrugged her off.

"I don't want to."

"You have to start school soon," her father said firmly.

Feeling it futile to resist, she finally consented. Her father relaxed, smiled, patted her on the head.

"What if they put me in a comer?"

"They won't if you behave yourself," her father guaranteed.

"What if that naughty boy bothers me, or eats my cookies?"

Her father broke out in laughter as he glanced at Lena.

"He won't." Her father kept laughing. "I'll make sure."

Her father patted her thigh reassuringly. She sat still, feeling the car weave in and out of lanes. She took a deep breath. If the bully ate her cookies, she would bite him on his cheek too, but much harder.

"How long do I stay in Kindergarten, Dadee?" she inquired.

"Until you start first grade, hon."

"How long is that?"

"Only four months. That's not long."

Four months. That length of time seemed like an eternity. But she could make it if she had too. The idea of having so little to say in the matter threw her into a mood of annoyance. She wondered if her mother would he happy to get rid of her so she could watch her horror movies in peace. Her father took his foot off the gas pedal and the car's left flasher started winking green, and Lena started winking back and laughing.

"School's fun," her father coaxed. "You'll love it."

Her father cut off the engine, as they rolled into the yard of their house.

"School is for your own good, Lena."

She unfastened her safety belt and got out of the car, wishing she were as cold and unfeeling as that hunk of iron car in which she rode.

"Angel, how did it go?" her mother asked.

Her stomach seemed queasy as she imagined a long stay at the kindergarten. Her mother held her hands on her hips, waiting for an answer. She deliberately ignored her mother, to irritate her. Was this abusive and hostile woman who would mistreat her at any moment her mother? She was probably better off at the kindergarten than with her mother. Strangely she appraised her mother in a way she could not explain, but in a way which seemed to coincide with the way her father appraised her. Now she regarded her mother in the same disgusted manner that her father regarded her. As she stood on the porch, she wished her mother would just leave her alone even though she had relented in mistreating her.

"You're not goin' to talk to Mommy?" her mother asked in an imitation of concern.

"She's still in shock," her father said. "But she'll adjust."

Lena walked into the house behind her parents, the screen door closing by itself. She could see that her mother was still waiting for an answer.

"She loves the school," her father smiled, hoping to give Lena the idea that that was the best thing that was about to happen in her whole life.

"Great, now I can have some time for myself," her mother blurted happily.

"I love school?" she mumbled quietly, thoughtfully.

"Jim, stop pushing the school off on her," her mother argued.

"Preschooling is important for her debut into first grade, Crystal," her father explained. "Gives her a chance to get out of the house. My putting words in her mouth will be support for her when she goes."

"She's only four," her mother argued again.

"So?" her father suddenly raged, then quickly smiled, frowning. "Crystal, don't try'n defeat the purpose." He shook his head anxiously. "You're confused, Crystal. You're in a

EYES OF A CHILD   65

different time zone.

Lena thought that her mother was sheltering her only so she could be in opposition with her father. She believed it strongly. Her mother's senseless disputes with her father told on her. Her shameless actions lacked reasoning and substance and revealed a destructive personality that could destroy her father. It was such a barbaric mentality, yet she was so proud of it. Her mother had the power to pull her family down with her, to destroy them along with herself. And Lena disliked the fact that she was being used as a pawn.

"A little lost in life, Crystal," her father complained.

Lena could see simpleness on her mother's face and she could tell that she was ready to argue.

"How dare you attack me like that?" her mother said.

Lena hurried to the refrigerator, bubbling with anxiety. Her father sat close to the TV holding his tongue. After a while her mother realized she could not provoke an argument, so she wandered off in the house. Lena wanted to get away from the headaches she often got from her mother. Her father appeared in the kitchen and hugged her softly.

"Lena," he spoke sincerely, "you will some day realize life's a learning process from the cradle to the grave. Every day you live you learn something new if you realize it or not." His tone sounded sad. "Some learn faster than others because some had a better upbringing than others. What you learn and practice and become is environmental to a high degree. In slums kids learn the ethics of street life, the pain, defeat, tragedy. If you hang with this type of garbage it's a certain ride to hell." Her father's tone changed to a muffled scream gilded with hate. "In rich families kids learn the ways of the good life of pleasure, victory, and power. They learn the ways to rule over the poor people, to keep them down so they themselves can stay up, but the poor have been blind too long to see that. They allow the rich to subjugate us, enslave us, abuse us for their own pleasure and benefit. The only way out for them is education, but they're too blind and ignorant to see that too. Your mother is, unfortunately, an ideal example of this. So the hate she learned from a hateful society is unleashed on her family and we all have to suffer for something we did not do or cause. You will some day see that what I'm saying is right before your eyes. All you have to do is open them to see for yourself, Lena."

"I know," she lied. Lena pondered, wishing she understood. But she had absorbed too much in too short a time. The thought of kids being rich or poor appeared foreign to her, but she was worried that since she did not understand maybe she was blind and ignorant like the people that her father was talking about. She had never thought of the rich or poor, but now she was thinking about it in a confused way and it bothered her.

"The rich hate us and they prove it by the way they treat us," her father ranted in his serious tone. "They keep us on food stamps and welfare instead of giving us jobs and education. That's the same as giving us the scraps and bones that fall from their tables. They actually live off us; the rich become rich by living off the poor, by exploiting their ignorance, stealing their pennies, and forcing them into legalized slave wages. They hate anyone who wants an education because their wealth could be threatened; anyone who wants to rise from poverty because they don't want to share; anyone who's aware of their conniving and deceit because they want all the power. That's why you're starting school so soon, so you'll become aware of that treachery in our society at an early age, and may not fall victim to it like I did and millions of others."

"Awright," she agreed, still unable to understand.

Her father's bitterness vanished as swiftly as it appeared and she wondered if he had really been bitter at all. He smiled sweetly at her. She was much too young to fully understand.

"When you're mature you'll understand," her father promised.

"When's that, Dadee?"

"Not sure, hon. Maybe when you're five or six. But time will tell," her father explained. "Education usually helps, but I do know a lot of educated fools. Most of them come out of poverty though." He stared at the floor then at Crystal and then back to Lena. "I'm an educated fool," he confessed. "I let the rich defeat me and let the poor crush me. They're both no good."

Lena's eyes widened. Educated fools? Impossible.

People who got educated could still be fools? The educated always read books and studied and the idea that they could still be fools gave her a tickling in her stomach that made her want to laugh.

"How come, Dadee?" she asked, squinting in confusion.

"Because the change is too much of a shock for them," her father said.

"You mean they can't cope with improvement?"

"Sometimes they can't," her father said. He always had answers to all of her questions. "They feel safe and contented living in a cesspool. There's lots of fun in the slum and a lot of misery, too. Once education helps them to become aware of life outside a slum they feel unsafe and out of place and immediately return."

"I'm going to school to get smart," Lena said when her mother came in the room.

"Your father talked you into it," her mother said with a contemptuous stare.

They were suddenly as loud as stiffs in a morgue.

Lena felt she was living in a dungeon and a lid blocked the top and blotted out her life. She sensed her mother was mad and an aura of madness seemed to dictate the household. She had a different image of her mother now. If her mother would hurt her, then she could not trust her. She felt sad and helpless, and there was nothing she could do to overcome her helplessness. She could not really pinpoint it but she felt that maybe her mother hated everybody.

"Keep your ears open and you'll learn," her father implied. "Intelligent people listen and stupid people talk. Be a listener and not a talker. Just make sure you listen to someone that's educated. You can't let the blind lead the blind or you'll become blinder."

"You're loony beyond help, Jim," her mother was really mad. "The educated know nothing and you know it, so why don't you just admit it? The uneducated knows everything and I can prove it, because the uneducated knows that too much reading makes people crazy like you." She sneered at her husband with a wrinkle of her nose. "And she doesn't understand what in hell you're talkin' about anyway."

"Someday she will," he smiled confidently. "Don't get trapped in that trend, like your mother did, that stupid people, because they talk so much, are smart. Stupid women listen to advice from the wrong people but reject the advice from the right people."

He looked over at Lena. "The dumb eat beans and Brussels sprouts and the smart eat steak and shrimp and black caviar."

"Mmmmm," Lena agreed, thinking of a juicy steak, of grilled shrimp soaked in garlic butter, of washing it down with ice cold Coca-Cola in a peaceful household that would not cause her indigestion.

Her mother's actions pleaded for a peaceful home, but she always compromised the peace with her desire for misery. Agitated, Lena prayed for deliverance from her mother, to clog her ears up, to hide somewhere, to find a way to escape from this horror of power struggle raging between her parents. It now appeared that her mother just talked to incense her father and her father sounded intelligent as he talked but sounded helpless as he argued. Family harmony seemed like something Lena seen on a cartoon show, a vivid image in her mind, but a vague possibility in her life. As she sat down on the floor to play with her toys, her father smiled, stroked her tumbling curls, and said:

"Don't worry, hon. Some people take a hostile stance if they feel they are not as intelligent as other people."

"Awright, Dadee," she smiled to hide her mood of vexation.

Burying herself in her toys, she lifted her head, when there was a hard knocking on the door.

"I'll be right back," her father promised. Her father peered through a windowpane, then smiled at Lena and winked. "It's your cousin, Lori Ann, Lena, and she's got Matthew with her."

Lena was happy and wanted to play with Matthew. It was okay with her father because Lori Ann was one of the few in her mother's family who did not try to make his life miserable. Shirley, DD, Nancy, Nanny, Dianna, all lived to torment her father.

"This is a bad time for her to pay a social visit. I'll tell her to bring back Matthew later," her father said.

"Awright," Lena said, still wanting to play with Matthew.

The misgivings and doubts she had regarded her mother with were coming back to light. Playing on the floor eating chewy Chips Ahoy, she watched her father talking to Lori Ann, and Matthew interrupting in toddler language. She had the urge to run outside and coddle Matthew. Then, Lori Ann, holding Matthew's hand, left and her father closed the door with a hint of cruelty on his face and called for her mother. Startled by a sudden facial change, Lena dropped her toys, knowing something new was stirring in the witch's brew. Her father's eyes were grim, dreamy, and it looked like something strange had drained his senses. She lost her appetite for her Chips Ahoy as she waited for the worst to erupt.

"She's dead," her father mumbled sarcastically, brutally.

"Who's dead?" her mother shrieked, rushing into the living room.

"Your mother dropped dead on her face on her kitchen floor," her father gloated. "Your detective brother who hates me broke down the door and called the hearse. He rode to the morgue with her."

"Oh, God!" her mother mumbled in shock. "My poor old mother."

"Why did she die?" Lena asked.

"Why do you think?" her father answered with brutal sarcasm. Then straight faced. "She had a heart attack." He looked about anxiously. "What a relief!" He laughed and taunted Crystal. "Want me to go to the morgue and see if I can bring her back to life?"

"You bastard," Crystal censured him. "My lonely mother died and you think it's a joke."

"Dadee!" Lena said. She was confused and wanted him to tell her what was happening.

"Look. I'm not wrong for treating her like she treated me." The anxious voice was wary, vengeful. "I'm aware of how bad I sound. I'm glad she's dead. Of course I feel terrible that you'll be suffering. My daughter's more important to me than your mother, Crystal. It's your mother and you don't want to hear that. But look. Remember how your mother tried to steal Lena from me by going through you, and when that failed she got you to turn Lena against me, and when that succeeded, she still wasn't finished with me, and she called the police to have me thrown out of her house with your instigation. So how can I miss her? When someone attacks my family, I want vengeance no matter how I get it. Nature balanced out the scale of justice, turned on your mother, and left her dead. You don't get away with nothin'. I see it as a blessing. Your mother's gone and I'm safe with my Lena."

"You're wrong," Crystal cried in agony.

"No I'm not. Nature took its course, and I'm happy." He shook his head, emphasizing his true feelings. "I believe her days were cut short because of her meddling in private affairs. But she was too ignorant to live and let live. She never believed she was ever going to die. I can only imagine what she's thinking now. I bet if she could live her life again she would be real nice and sweet to me."

"She wasn't bothering no one," Crystal grieved.

"Just me," her father said in judgment. "That fluffy old goat was nothin' more than a troublemaker, and since she's dead you're dumb enough to make it look like she was a saint. What fateful event brought me in contact with your mother I'll never know." Lena could see that his hate was so intense that he was trembling, sweating, and dead set on never changing his beliefs. She thought she detected sadness, happiness and relief in his voice all at the same time.

She realized that her father hated her grandmother intensely, but did not quite understand why.

"You just hated her," her mother accused. "She never bothered you."

"Of course she never bothered me. She only separated me from Lena for a whole year, you fucking idiot," her father screamed.

"You brought that on your ownself," her mother said.

"That's the funniest joke I ever heard," her father laughed. "It's a lame defense, Crystal."

"You're just hateful, Jim," her mother stressed through flowing tears. "And you know you're hateful."

"Just to people that hate me," her father confessed.

Lena now realized that her father hated her mother more than he had hated her grandmother and held her mother responsible for her grandmother's actions.

"My lonely old mother," her mother cried hysterically now.

"Yes, your lonely old mother," her father mocked laughingly.

Her father's heartless attack on her grandmother had left Lena suspended in confusion; in that attack was brutal revenge, but also dreaded revenge. She automatically sensed that her father, soaked with fear as he announced his true feelings, was defying that fear and that was what impelled him to condemn as he confessed. She also sensed that her father's security could be confirmed only by his gloating at the death of her grandmother, which definitely proved that he was trapped in a feared but unconscious insecurity.

"Your mother died for me, Crystal," her father stressed. He smiled at Lena, then glared at her mother, retreated to the kitchen and took a can of diet Coke out of the refrigerator, popped the lid, and sipped it heartily.

Lena watched her mother's stare assessing her puzzled look.

"That was your Nanny, Lena."

"Why talk to her like that, Crystal?"

"Because she's gonna know the truth," her mother cried.

"Good idea," her father agreed. He jolted his head toward Lena. "Hon, when you were born your grandmother helped us take care of you, and in the meantime tried to run me off and keep you all to herself. She wanted you to be a backstabber and sneak like the rest of the women in her family, but when I resisted your mother and all her woman relatives teamed up against me. It was a nightmare that haunts me to this day."

Her father's sincerity sent a flash of anger through her mind.

"You're a liar," her mother screamed.

"Am I, Crystal? I haven't even dreamed of telling Lena the whole truth. I wouldn't hurt my own flesh'n blood."

"But you're hurting me."

"Crystal, Lena is my life and I'm not going to tolerate you as an accessory to take her away from me. Is that clear?"

Her mother commenced her hysterical crying and wished him dead.

"I'm going, Dadee," Lena crackled sadly. The awareness of her parent's hate toward each other had compounded her confusion and she could feel sadness tearing at her heart. "You and Mommy fight too much." Her father did not reply as she made her way to the door of the living room and leaned her head on the metallic framing. She felt lost, empty, abandoned, and terribly scared, even after her father had pampered her.

"Crystal, have I made myself clear?" her father said in a concerned, nervous voice.

"All you've done is made me hate you more," she gasped, her eyes full of hate and still wishing him dead.

"That's no surprise," he said gravely.

"You'll be sorry," her mother promised.

Lena stared pensively at a row of streetlights that gleamed like mint copper pennies through the hot summer morning. She knew that her father had suffered at some time. She was certain that only people who suffer profoundly could malign the dead with such cruelty.

Lena's father touched her shoulders gently. She could not stand to hear her mother crying anymore.

"It happens everyday," her father said in a regretful voice.

"I don't like it, Dadee," Lena whispered.

"I'm afraid it's something you'll just have to accept, hon," he answered.

"Awright." She accepted her fate.

Her mother suddenly appeared beside them. Her mother,

shaking and still crying, was glaring at her father.

"I hope you die," she groaned in despair.

"Me too," her father said wryly, a haunted look on his face.

"Take her to death with you," her mother said, shaking a frightening finger at Lena. A second later, with even a more stricken look on her face, she cried louder, mumbling. "You bastard, just go by yourself and leave us alone."

He stared at her mother in a weird way that Lena could not understand.

"Sure," he said sarcastically.

Lena realized she was pitifully trapped in her parents' nerve racking nightmares of dispute. She turned her head and continued looking out at the coppery streetlights, shedding a waste of light in the brightening daylight.

For the rest of the day she felt nauseated, irritated, intimidated, and unable to muster the incentive to play with her toys.

Chapter Nine

To Lena's relief the arguments over Nanny's death vanished as quickly as they had arisen. Nanny's five children assumed that death was the decision of Mother Nature handing down what is always for the best. Jim apologized for his blatant remarks about Nanny, but proclaimed that it had had a wonderful impact upon Lena by teaching her the evils of in law life. Crystal encouraged her daughter to spite her father, to turn against him, for all his actions and words were of bad intent. The following weeks that encroached on her life, Lena's fears of her personal safety were soothed more from brain congestion than from the tentative ebbing of contention between her parents. Though Nanny had been disliked and snubbed by Jim, the viewing of her bloated corpse instilled a sudden change in him, and, after the funeral, he never again referred to her with harsh resentment.

May of Lena's fifth year did not usher her into kindergarten as had been planned. Crystal's opposition at this particular time overruled Jim's wish, but Lena was allowed more freedom outdoors. Lena soon developed a pattern of looking about suspiciously as if expecting something evil to happen, a practice that magnified her slum conditioning, and which proved that she was adjusting properly to the environment. As always a suspicious look accompanied anything she did, a suspicion induced by a treacherous upbringing in a blighted home life. But everything was for a reason and fate was just acting accordingly.

Hardened by continual hostility, she assumed that that was the normal way parents prepared their kids for the hardships of life. She learned to enjoy a life of hostility, hatred, blight, with no pleasure in sight. Her life was flooded with abuse, neglect, languor, worry, and she realized that her mother was the principal in bestowing it upon her and now Lena planned to keep it like that.

She thrived in a broken house in which morals were stressed and never followed, in which abuse was practiced but always denied. She learned quickly the connotation of Crystal violating family taboos. Crystal now appeared to her as a volatile mother who basked in life's miseries; a social outcast whose daily practice was ignorance. To Lena, this description of Crystal could not have been more accurate. Granted, Crystal did speak of delight in life, but concentrated on how fate had wrongfully bestowed upon her an ill-fated life, and she knew that her day of deliverance was as remote as a dream come true. Lena would criticize Crystal in her mind, for she was certain that the rest of the world was similar to hers. Lena had attempted to make some sense between Crystal and the fantasy life about which she spoke, but when failing to do so she would smile sadly, then fill with compassionate understanding.

"Something might be wrong with Mother!" she exclaimed.

While lolling underneath a shade tree in the heat, Lena saw DJ hurrying for the Majik Market in long, anxious strides. Lena waved at him and he met her on the corner.

"Lena, I got something to show you," DJ said wonderfully.

"Really? Let's see it!" Lena said.

"Yep, you're going to love it," DJ taunted her.

Lena grabbed DJ's wrist, holding him in place so that he would not get away if he changed his mind. A sly look masked his face.

"Show me, DJ. Hurry up," Lena pleaded anxiously.

"Slow down," DJ urged. "Relax a moment." He took in a chest full of air as he boasted. "I got it all by myself."

"Got what?"

"You'll never believe it," DJ laughed.

"I won't?" Lena said, suspecting trouble, but keeping it to herself in case she had to steer clear of him.

He jammed his dirty hand into his pants pocket and extracted a crisp one dollar bill.

"I stole this out of my Mom's purse."

Lena stiffened, then felt sick with fear. She could see DJ's mother taking a stick and beating the daylights out of him, and her getting beat next for just knowing about it.

"Why?"

"Why? So I can buy an ice cream cone."

"Bad boy, DJ," Lena snapped, heading back in the house.

"Hey, Lena," DJ's face filled with concern. "I'm only fibbin'."

"I bet your mommy's gonna beat you," Lena said, ignoring DJ's defense.

"Huh, uh, because I didn't steal it from 'er."

"You swear to God and hope to die?"

"I swear to God, but I don't know about hoping to die."

Lena was amazed how DJ could lie with a straight face. "You stole it from your mother," she said again.

"No I didn't," DJ defended. "She said I could take it."

"Are you tellin' the truth?"

"I have no reason to lie."

"See, DJ, I don't play with kids that steal!"

"Neither do I."

Lena searched his face seeking the truth.

"Awright, DJ, but you shouldn't lie!" Lena scolded him.

"But," DJ mimicked a big kid as he stood in front of Lena. "I just wanted you to think I was big by saying I stole the dollar from my mother. I wouldn't do that. She probably would beat me. She knows that I know better 'n that. But I did take it out of her purse. But she knew about it

"Good boy, DJ." Lena was happy, but still wary of his sudden change of story.

"You want an ice cream?" DJ asked. "We can go over to Majic Market. I'll buy."

"No, I'm not allowed to go across the street."

"You can sneak over there," DJ suggested.

"But my daddy said no," Lena wailed her refusal. "Cars are always racin' up and down the street."

"He won't know 'less you tell 'im."

"I'm not your best friend no more, DJ," Lena sputtered.

"You ain't nothin' but a sissy baby!"

The ridicule made her face feel hot.

"I'm no sissy," Lena said, staring.

Silently DJ secreted the dollar back into his pocket then strolled off for the convenience store.

Anger arose in Lena and she started after him.

"My dad won't know 'less you tell 'im," Lena sang in a justifying tone.

DJ smiled delightedly as he saw Lena trailing behind him.

"That's right," DJ agreed.

At the store Lena sulked about DJ luring her away, and worried about the probability that her father would be very disappointed in her for crossing the dangerous street without an adult escort. While sucking on a two stick Popsicle under the chilling air blowing by the store's air conditioner, she saw her twin cousins, Billy and Dawn, who came into the store,

EYES OF A CHILD 79

shirtless and barefooted. Disgusted by their grubby profiles, and the fact that their familics had split up after a sudden death in the family, she was hesitant to even speak to them. Mommy had accused Aunt Patti of killing her brother, Uncle William, and then the feud started. But she gave in. After all they were family and she still liked Aunt Patti, even though she was nasty to Mommy.

"DJ got me this cherry Popsicle," Lena spoke in a sparkling, friendly tone, "and it tastes good too."

Sneers screened their faces. Billy, the leader, glared down at Lena, his sneer getting worse, ugly, as he braced himself in a defiant, hostile stance.

"That's expected," Billy explained. "You spoiled little brats always out beggin' for a freebie."

"That sure is the truth," Dawn said bluntly. "Our Mama never let's us beg."

"You two just jealous," DJ said defending Lena.

"You think DJ's right, Lena?" Billy questioned with an aggressive look.

"I don't think nothin '," Lena was hostile.

Billy looked surprised at that. Dawn watched him carefully. DJ laughed.

"She ain't even in first grade yet," DJ said.

"I knew she was just a snotty nose little baby," Billy whined nastily. "But I still wouldn't have got the baby beggar no Popsicle no how. I'd make the brat buy 'er own."

Billy's sister and DJ just listened, wondering what was next. Lena noticed their stern faces set with a pretense of superiority and she wished to never see them again.

"Billy, now I know you're just a jealous fool," she said flatly.

"Think what you want." Billy coughed. "I ain't got no time to play with no squirt. I have better things to do."

"Like what?" Lena asked with cutting sarcasm.

"None of your beeswax," Dawn added support for her brother.

"Aw, leave 'er alone," DJ urged. "I 'tole ya she wasn't even in first grade."

Lena had stood her ground in her encounter with her neighborhood cousins and she was unsure if this was good or bad. She was hoping that she had taken the right approach. Was her defiance of her cousins' ridicule proper?

"Yeah, why bother?" Billy said, trying to sound big.

"That's right," Dawn chimed in.

"Ha, ha," Lena laughed. She was mocking them now.

"Maybe you'll leave 'er alone now," DJ hoped. "Fightin' with a baby is like fightin' with your parents. You can't win."

Lena felt confident as she looked at Billy and Dawn's pathetic, dirty faces.

"Listen to 'im!" Lena urged laughingly. "Not because I'm a baby, but because I'm big too."

"Okay," Billy interrupted Lena. "One last thing though. I don't want you beggin' on DJ for freebies anymore, you hear?"

"Get lost, Billy," Lena whined angrily. "You ain't my mother."

DJ flashed a big smile. Billy and Dawn stared in surprise at Lena's mood.

"Let's go," Dawn insisted, tossing her blond hair in a swirl.

"Yeah," Billy agreed. He and Dawn moved to the candy rack, and both grabbed king sized Snicker bars.

Yeah, Lena smiled, keep eating those big yummy candy bars. Eat them all day long, idiots, and don't forget to eat one right before bedtime, and don't brush your teeth either, so your teeth will rot out just like mine. If you idiots run out of money I'll buy you some more. Lena felt very good about herself and her cousins now. She stared out through the swinging door to her shabby house and thought that she had better be getting home.

"Bye, kiddie," Billy said as he and Dawn paid for their candy bars and walked out ripping open the wrappers.

Lena was glad they left as she turned her attention back to her Popsicle. Good riddance. She now thought of getting back home before her parents found that she had wandered off. Her cousins had caused a strange heaviness to settle in her stomach. She saw DJ smiling slyly.

"You showed them," DJ said proudly.

"I sure did," Lena nodded in deep glee.

"You know they're both nine years old," DJ spoke admiringly, "and you outdone 'em both?"

"See, DJ, they big shots," Lena joked. "You know, real proud, but I wouldn't know of what?"

DJ nodded his agreement.

"I gotta go," Lena said anxiously.

"See ya later."

Lena dumped the rest of her Popsicle into the store garbage can and looked both ways before darting across the street with her head tilted slightly down. The soles of her tiny red tennis shoes made a crunching sound as she touched the gravel sidewalk. She was not back underneath the shade trees for more than a second before her father appeared in his pajamas.

"Where have you been?" her father asked tiredly.

"Over there," Lena pointed at the store.

"Don't ever do that again," he said, shaking his head in a negative manner.

"She's getting to be a big girl," her mother opposed. "She won't get run over crossing that busy street. Those drunks around here drink and drive all the time and they ain't hit nobody yet."

Her mother's stupidity had her father trapped as usual. Stupidity must run in the family; just look at her mother, Billy and Dawn, they were all related. Lena did understand her father was concerned enough to be angered by her disobedience and now she was sorry; she never appreciated a drop of protection which her mother only offered in defiance of her father's wishes for her safety. She knew that her mother was slowly forcing on her her own beliefs, habits, actions, that had bad intent, endless conflict, a troubling personality that her father vainly tried to prevent from being infused into her upbringing.

Chapter Ten

As she sat on the floor two feet from the TV screen with her bunny rabbit and a big glass of apple juice to watch her favorite show, Frazzle Rock, Lena heard a faint tapping at the front door. She wiped her moist hands on her clothes, put her bunny in a sitting position, and went in search of her mother.

She had been warned by her father to never answer the door unless he or Crystal was with her. She went to the back porch and her mother leaned busily over a rumbling washing machine.

"Mommy, someone's at the door!"

Crystal lifted her head, staring. She pulled the switch and the washer groaned and shook before coming to a jerking stop. Crystal's eyes glared and she looked like she was about to start screaming.

"I'm busy, Lena," Crystal snapped.

"Someone's knocking at the door."

"Go see who it is," Crystal meanly encouraged.

She stepped back and moved for the door. Lena was surprised to see a rugged black form standing in front of the flimsy screen door.

"What do you want, Man?"

"I haven't eatin' for a whole two days, sweetie. Can you let me in to eat?" the stranger asked.

"Huh?" Lena was uncertain if she had heard correctly.

"Your mama home, little girl?"

He grabbed at the door knob.

Lena sensed danger and banged the inside wooden door shut with a lightning instinct. The automatic lock snapped in place.

"Bad man," Lena hollered.

"Aw, open up," he said real sweetly.

There was danger in the man's tone.

"No, no, no. Tell my Mommy on you."

Lena turned and, with the black man peeking in through the side windowpane, hurried madly for her mother, stepping over disarrayed household objects and breathing rapidly reentered the laundry room and stood anxiously next to her mother.

"Mommy. Mommy." She motioned toward the front of the house.

"You act like you're scared of something," Crystal noticed.

Ignoring the heat of the clothes dryer and the hum of electric appliances, repelling bleach fumes and the stale smell of fabric softener, Lena tried to explain to mother in a low tone of voice.

"Lena, I can't understand a word you're saying," she said negligently.

More vague mumbling followed.

"All right, Angel!" Crystal said. "Let's go see what's wrong."

Lena was on her mother's heels and when they reached the kitchen and could see the door Lena yelled.

"Go home, bad man!"

Crystal flinched when Lena yelled.

"Shut up," Crystal scolded.

Lena felt her confidence shatter and wondered why her

EYES OF A CHILD 85

mother had not taken her belligerent tone as a sign of danger. But as they reached the door she was braver than before since she had her mother at her side and she again cried against her mother's will.

"Go home, bad man!" She looked up at Crystal. "He's still at the door, Mommy."

Crystal glanced at the shut door then around the room but all was intact.

"You're as paranoid as your dad!"

"Huh, uh," Lena said tauntingly, confidently and pointed.

A shiny pitch black face filled the square of windowpane and, as Crystal inched closer for a better look, it suddenly disappeared. She moved to the door and opened a gap in the cobwebby window blind, and looked out. She was staring with wrinkled brow at the shirtless, muscled physique of a black man who looked ready to flee.

"You want something, mister?" she asked in an angry voice. It's not like she hated black men; she had a black boyfriend in her teenage years; it was just she did not want any strange, abusive men around her daughter, so she could do all the abusing.

"I'm starving, ma'am."

"So?"

"Can you give me a bite to eat, please."

"Look, mister. This ain't no cafeteria. Go to work. Everybody's starving. With all those muscles you got you sure don't look underfed. Now get lost and don't you ever let me see you lookin' in my window again, or I'll blow your brains out, and afterwards call the police, you hear, mister?"

"Oh, yessum," he stressed and hurried off.

They watched him disappear down the road. Lena wondered how he had happened to stumble across their house when there was so many other houses around. She could feel that something was bothering her mother but she quickly dispelled it from her mind.

"I told you, Mommy."

"I know."

"Who was he?"

"Nobody that's goin' to bother us."

"Awright," Lena said drenched with fear.

Lena sensed suspicion within her mother's own accusing malady.

"Where 'd he go, Mommy?"

Anxious cursing flared up in Crystal.

"Away and he better stay that way if he knows what's good for 'im!" Crystal said in a threatening gesture.

"You see how strong that man was, Mommy?"

"I seen how strong he was. It doesn't mean nothing," Crystal assured her. "I'd put a bullet in him as quick as I can blink."

Lena's emotions were running wild. That man was really brave. Then her imagination ran wilder and she imagined him forcing his way inside and overpowering her, taking her away before anybody, including her father, could rescue her. A veil of dew appeared on her face, and her trembling hands wiped it away. She was viewing the reality of the world that lurked outside, the world into which she knew she would someday be trapped. Her mind probed further into that world and she immediately fell into gloominess. To be trapped forever in that world guaranteed perpetual misery. She blinked her eyes slowly; she did not quite understand why all incidents in life seem to slide away from safety, security, happiness. She moved breathlessly to the door and turned the knob to make sure it was locked. She suddenly felt that she wanted to remain in her own little world instead of being cast into the other.

Her analytical mind stopped exploring the realities of the future and she noticed an eerie spookiness blanketed the house as if that man was hiding inside. She started breathing quietly in case he was inside, but not so she could catch him, but so he would not catch her. She was terrified of living in her own home, but she felt better when she heard the rats scratching inside the walls. She leaned her face on the cool glass of the windowpane and stared out into the other world. Her wet little tongue darted out and licked at the mildewed glass, which made her feel safe and smug in her own private cesspool.

"What are you looking for?" Crystal asked.

Lena's body jolted nervously as she was so engrossed in her thoughts.

"You scared me, Mommy," Lena said with a twitching smile.

"I'll be in the back if you want me," Crystal said.

"Awright."

A while later she was happy to see her father's white Camaro pull into the yard. Good. She would tell him about that man. She tried to reach the safety lock, but it was too far beyond the grasp of her hand. She heard his keys rattling, and then the door swung open.

"Dadee," Lena happily sang.

"Lena, baby," Jim happily returned.

Lena's smile vanished and she grew serious.

"Dadee, you know what?" Lena said hesitantly.

"Wait, hon," Jim said seriously. "Where's your Mom? I got to speak to her. It's important."

"She's in the back washing clothes."

Jim took hold of Lena's hand and sought out Crystal.

"Crystal," he called.

"What are you doin' home so early?" she sounded surprised.

His high-strung mood caused him to almost stutter.

"Never mind that," Jim insisted. "A rapist killer escaped

from the maximum security detention facility here in Lauderdale this morning. He's armed and extremely dangerous. The Fort Lauderdale Police Department warned the neighboring residents to remain inside and keep their doors locked."

Crystal's face turned pale.

"Really?" she said.

Lena's eyes darted in surprise to her mother's suddenly pale face.

"He's believed to be somewhere in the neighborhood?" Crystal whispered. She imagined herself being attacked and beaten, raped, maybe even murdered while Lena helplessly watched on in horror.

"That's right," Jim assured.

"Dadee, what's a rapist killer?" Lena was puzzled.

"It's not important at this moment," Jim said as he smiled at Lena.

She grabbed his hand and started pulling on it.

"Come on, Dadee. What is that?"

Her father did not answer her right away. He kept shifting in an anxious mood as he looked intently at her mother, and glanced a couple of times her way. Her mother was not saying or doing anything.

"Please, Dadee. Pretty please with a cherry on the top," she shouted and grinned.

"It's a bad, bad boy," her father finally answered.

"Oh, awright," Lena was satisfied.

They all walked out of the back room and into the kitchen.

"Will you tell me why you're acting so strange, Crystal?"

Crystal felt nervous, her mind kept touching on how she had told Lena to go and answer the door all by herself fully knowing that that was bad judgment. What if that man had been the fugitive? Worry of telling that to Jim kept her silent. She felt revulsion toward herself for her disregard for Lena's safety. She felt torn between concern and neglect. She looked nervously at Jim, sensing that he was aware that something was wrong and that it involved Lena. Would Jim be mad at her for ordering Lena to a duty that required adult supervision? Should she be truthful and confess? Maybe, but first she would be deceptive and pry for information before revealing a truth that could have an adverse effect upon her.

"What color was he?" Crystal asked suddenly.

"White," Jim lied because Crystal looked like she was scheming about something.

The time felt right and Crystal poured out a confession.

"Wow, am I glad," Crystal admitted, grateful for Jim's relaxed mood. "I was afraid you were goin' to say black because some scared looking black man was at the door asking for a free meal and, you know, when I told him to beat it he just took off. Lena seemed worried and came and got me, even slammed the door in his face. You know, Jim, she's gettin' to be a big girl, that's why I let her do things on her own."

Jim did not say anything for several minutes, but his eyes never left her face. He glanced at Lena and his eyes softened, but hardened again when he looked back at Crystal. The channel seven news brief with Rick Sanchez had announced that the escapee had been a Negro. He now held in him the belief that Crystal was an idiot for a mother, and if he had another chance in life, he would not want her to be the mother of his kid. He was extremely concerned for Lena's safety.

"Yeah, she's learning," Jim suddenly said calmly. "How long ago did this man come here?"

"About ten minutes ago," she said and she shrugged her shoulders. "Why?"

"Just wondering," Jim said, smiling.

"Something wrong?" Crystal took a Kool cigarette from the package.

"Nothing at all," Jim said. "I got to be back at work pretty soon."

Jim moved away with Lena at his heels. He hated the smell of tobacco on Crystal's hands, face, breath, more than he hated her stupidity and selfishness and recklessness with Lena's security and happiness. The fumes from those cigarettes would kill them all before a criminal got to them.

He doesn't suspect a thing, she told herself confidently. He's stupid. All that college he had made him stupider than had he not went to college at all. Lena would someday understand what was wrong with her father.

Lena held his hand now as they moved into the next room to the phone where he tapped three digits. Lena watched him closely. He glared at Crystal when she came in from the kitchen with her lit cigarette dangling from her lips, as he explained to a police detective that he suspected the rapist killer had moments ago paid a visit to his home. Lena gasped and huddled between his legs as Crystal's jaw dropped in shock and the cigarette fell to the floor.

Chapter Eleven

While an unexpected burst of conflict over Nanny's death recurred one day as Lena and her parents were at Fort Lauderdale beach, the lifeguards gave a warning shout that a tidal wave was thundering toward shore and Lena jumped up screeching as more excitement had entered her blighted upbringing. As she spotted the glistening tidal wave approaching, she started pointing, laughing, jumping up and down as her parents stopped their arguing, grabbed her by the arms and made a mad dash for safety along with hundreds of sightseers and sunbathers. It hit the shoreline with a thundering crash, scaring the tourists and ripping down all the coconut palms lining the beach. Most had been pulled from their roots and as the water receded the undertow was so strong it took many of the trees with it.

Then, an hour later, when everybody was back on the beach and thought they were safe, a tornado barreled in off the ocean roaring like a freight train, lashing the flatland with the blackest of funnels, and damaging many of the fancy restaurants and tourists shops on Las Olas Boulevard. In its wake came pelting hail and strong winds that howled through the streets and rattled windows of expensive hotels and scratched the paint on Mercedes and Porsches and Rolls Royce's parked along the streets.

Then a month later an unseasonable hurricane season struck at Fort Lauderdale, and brought about yet another encounter with dread in Lena's turbulent life. A category four hurricane stormed across the city, lashing at everything unfortunate enough to get caught in its path and producing green and blue flutters of lightning that hovered close to the rooftops for seconds at a time. It unleashed an eerie howling of wind with gusts of over a hundred and sixty miles an hour, razing entire neighborhoods and causing scores of deaths, and knocking out power plants and telephone lines that took months to repair. Its fitful winds and lashing rain had damaged the roads and walks, making the asphalt crack and crumble, and ruining the structures of most of the historical shacks overlooking the marble mansions of Fort Lauderdale Beach.

"These storms are horrible," Jim said in a deep mood of disgust, "it ruins the sales at my Seven Eleven. Storm or shine, the customers will still spend their money if they can get to the store. But when sales are down, I make less money and raise more questions from my bosses. They label you a thief before they catch you and convict you before they try you."

Crystal, as usual, was plotting against the family.

"When a hurricane hits this viciously, it's a sign that more might be comin'," she mumbled strangely to Lena.

"Another hurricane, Mommy?" Lena asked, terrified all over again.

"Those hurricanes can destroy us," she said deliberately to scare her daughter, even though Lena was already shaking. "You've only been through one hurricane and you seen how many people died."

"It can even kill us?" Lena asked, trying not to cry. If the last hurricane did not get her maybe nothing would.

"You got it," she answered with an ugly twist of her nose.

Lena went along with her mother, feeling that something

EYES OF A CHILD 93

was not right with her answer. If her mother was hoping to scare her she was doing a good job. Tornadoes were exciting and so were tidal waves, but not hurricanes; they pounded at your house all night long and could take the roof off and carry you away. Finally she wanted to ignore her mother, even though she acted like she was agreeing with her, but she was wondering why her mother spoke like that. Her conversations always lacked substance and logic.

"Well, Mommy, should I be afraid?" Lena asked. She wished her father had not left for work; his presence alone always strengthened her spirit.

"You better be afraid, if you keep hangin' with your father," she said, hostility. "He'll take you to your death."

"But, Mommy, I love Dadee," Lena protested, then lowered her head sadly.

"Don't contradict me," Crystal reproved her. "Your mother always knows best."

Lena fell silent, seeing that the irrationality her mother used contained no sense. Was her mother intentionally trying to scare her? She stared at her mother and wondered confusedly about her logic. The look in her mother's eyes showed Lena that she liked to agitate emotions within her. But why would she do this?

"You're right, Mommy," Lena said softly, obediently. "You probably do know everything." Her father had told her stupid people liked to be flattered and that was why she flattered her mother.

"Good girl, Angel!" her mother mumbled, smiling at Lena pleasingly. "I knew that you knew that Mommy knows best."

"Should I stay only with you, Mommy?" Lena was testing her mother.

"I would think so," Crystal said.

"Mommy, why do you hate Dadee?" Lena asked slyly.

"That's the second time you've pried into my private life,"

Crystal fumed. "It's none of your business why I hate him. So stop it."

Sad anger overcame Lena as she faintly remembered the strange, pumping man and her mother's glistening buttocks.

"You mean about that man friend of yours, Mommy?" Lena inquired.

Lena's day was ruined when her mother suddenly yanked painfully on her hair. She grabbed her mother's hands with all her strength, but could not break her grip.

"I told you not to ever mention that again," Crystal punished her, still yanking hard on her hair

Lena was unable to bear the pain and broke into sobbing when a fistful of hair came out by the roots This was the only time she had lost so much hair in so short a time. Would her mother start mistreating her again? She left her mother's presence as her mother held a handful of her hair.

"Lena, you made me do it," Crystal screamed.

She kept crying, holding her head.

"But I'm sorry, Angel! I still love you!"

Lena could feel thinning in her scalp. She hated to fight her mother, but if she did not she would be bald. Later, she probably would not, but now she had to or else she would lose more hair. The yanking had left a bald spot on her scalp. She finally got to her bedroom away from her mother's vicious hands.

She always pulls out my hair, Lena thought sadly.

Then she heard her mother's swishing feet entering the bedroom. As Crystal stood before her, Lena ignored her, rubbing at her eyes.

"Angel," Crystal said in a polite, apologizing tone.

"What?" Lena whined

"Mommy's man friend was supposed to be a secret, remember?" Crystal said politely.

"It was?" Lena asked, feeling bewildered.

"You must've forgotten," Crystal smiled.

Lena looked cautiously at her mother but remained angry. She felt now that her mother regretted pulling out her hair.

"It's okay though," Crystal said with concern. "It's easy to forget."

"I've got a bald spot on my head," Lena whimpered. "It don't feel good."

Crystal delicately hugged Lena then sat down, and pulled Lena into her lap.

"It's still raining," Crystal said, hoping to make her daughter relax.

"I'm scared of the rain," Lena countered. "Because you said a hurricane might kill us." She watched the rain swirl to the road like a white mist.

"You shouldn't be." Crystal sounded sincere. Her mood suddenly changed to anger. "Unless, you feel you should disobey me."

"I obey you," Lena said.

"Not when your father's around," Crystal complained moodily.

Lena patiently listened as Crystal spoke with subdued anger. She understood that Crystal wanted to make her commit herself to a guarantee that she would always obey her mother and always disobey her father, and that would be an ideal way to expand the opposition to her father.

"Mommy, I didn't know," Lena confessed to her. "I'll obey you too. I didn't know I had to say I'd obey."

"Angel, you just obey Mommy," Crystal said rudely. "Now I want Mommy's man friend to remain a secret forever, you hear?"

"Awright," Lena agreed, tears still in her eyes.

Feeling intensely restless on her mother's lap, she wished to be free, and standing in the rain under the velvety clouds, stomping bare-footed in the puddles and catching ringworms, laughing, watching cars speed by, and when her father was not watching, running across the street to get a Popsicle. Gingerly, she eased off Crystal's lap, but not to quick, for fear she might offend her and get more hair pulled out of her head.

"I'm gonna play with my toys, Mommy."

"Go ahead," Crystal replied. She got to her feet and left the room, walking like a zombie.

Happy now, she went to her toy chest and dug in. She pulled out books, dolls, cars, crayons, her floppy eared bunny rabbit, then finally, she got to her choo choo train. She sat on it and rolled to the window and gazed out at the falling rain.

Instinctively, Lena felt that someone was behind her. She spun about and saw her mother standing over her with a wooden paddle. Her excitement about another hurricane approaching had quickly turned to pain and was now turning to dread. Trembling, she cowered and pleaded to Crystal, whose intent vividly reflected abuse. She thought her mother was determined to break her spirit.

"No, don't," Lena begged, holding tightly to her choo choo train.

"Get up and bend over," her mother ordered. "I'm gonna give you something to help out your memory."

Lena's instincts urged her to flee, but Crystal's width blocked the exit to the bedroom. Then she thought to climb through a window, but her mother would be all over her before she pushed out the screen. She was trapped and had to face the facts. She blinked her eyes with the hope she would awaken from this nightmare. She had never been beaten with a paddle, only with Crystal's fists.

"No, don't," Lena cried.

Lena backed against the wall, waiting for her hateful mother to speak. She was drenched with dread. She should have never forgotten about the secret. Was Crystal really after her because she had forgotten not to mention her man friend....

"Hurry up, before I beat you where you sit," her mother growled.

"Don't, Mommy. Don't beat me," Lena cried out her heart. "I don't want to get a bad beating and get killed at five. Mommy, you might kill me."

"I just might," Crystal laughed. "Now let's get it over with and I might not kill you."

Lena inched next to Crystal, her dread making her feel dreamy. Suddenly, without a chance to resist, hands yanked down her pants.

"I cautioned you about being a bad girl a hundred times," her mother said.

"I'm not a bad girl, Mommy," Lena cried harder. "You told me that a hundred times. Please, don't beat me."

"You're getting a beatin' regardless," her mother said. "So, bend over the bed."

Trying to be brave, with heart racing, Lena crept to the bed, bent over, begging, trembling, ashamed of showing her naked buttocks in this helpless position. She felt degraded, humiliated, and hoped her mother would never say anything about this to anyone, especially to her father.

"Quit shaking," Crystal yelled cruelly.

Lena tightened up, her buttocks looking tense and red over the bed, her mind denying the abuse. She could not understand why her mother did not just pull out more of her hair. A crash of searing pain roared through her as the paddle hit her delicate rosy flesh. Then, in rapid succession, another and another crash of the paddle rattled her reasoning. The intensity of the pain rendered her numb, and her body jerked and tensed as stiff as a board. Finally, with all her strength, she forced out speech.

"Don't kill me, Mommy," Lena could barely moan.

"Stop faking," Crystal answered flatly.

Lena prayed fiercely for safety, for protection from her mother, for deliverance into a life of peace, but she knew this was something that only existed in her mind. Her aching buttocks made her think she was dying, made her legs feel like growing stumps of lead. She felt something strange happening to her, like her mind was leaving her body, and she saw this little helpless girl being brutally beaten by a ruthless mother who unquestionably loved her daughter. The pain became so unbearable now that she wondered if she was dreaming and did not seem to know where she was at. Then it dawned on her that her body was totally numb. The room was slowly closing in on her, and she felt confused, disoriented.

"I'll never let you disobey me again," Crystal promised, lashing at Lena's lacerated buttocks and laughing about it.

Deprived of speech, Lena only quivered as the beating went on.

"When I'm through with you, you'll be Mommy's little girl," Crystal said through tight, pursed lips. "Girl, I'm gonna make you my baby again."

A bottomless pit of blackness descended and swallowed Lena into its depths. She lost consciousness as she was falling and falling but never hit bottom. Then she awoke lying on her back to see her mother smiling down at her and pushing the paddle against her throat. Lena opened her mouth to scream, but she could not even talk.

She wanted to get up to run, but her beaten body felt paralyzed. Had she had the strength, she would have spit in her mother's face to spite her since she was still alive. She was suddenly aware that her mother was unclothed from the hips down. Softly, Crystal set down the paddle and stared at Lena and touched her and giggled. Lena was confused, puzzled, sickened. She tried to move away but her mother pushed her back.

"Angel, just relax. Mommy'll be through in a moment," Crystal mumbled quietly.

Lena's eyes welled with tears, and she noticed a penetrating pain in her head that radiated downward to her neck. She noticed her mother was touching herself and still giggling. Presuming what was happening was wrong, Lena lay back and wished for it to end. After her mother stopped her giggling, she finally let Lena sit up. Lena curled up and felt a shameness that baffled her still more.

"Angel, Mommy wants you to keep this a secret too, okay?" Crystal told her as she slipped back into her clothes. "If I was you I wouldn't want to tell anybody what happened."

"Mommy, why were you doing that to me?" Lena finally spoke but in a totally confused state. Somehow she knew that it was bad for her mother to do that to her.

"Stop inquiring. You're not supposed to question your mother!" Crystal was firm. Her words were charged with the sounds of guilt. "You should be ashamed of yourself for questioning Mommy."

Suddenly Lena was absorbed with guilt; a tormenting guilt that had settled deep in her mind and was getting more intense. How could she live with this guilt? How could she hide it forever? Her mind tumbled about and settled upon her mother's midsection. That's my Mommy's bad thing. And she realized it would always invoke fear in her.

"I won't question you no more, Mommy," Lena promised.

"Good girl, Angel," Crystal said, smiling. "I might even buy you a Popsicle. You wanna keep what happened our little secret, right?"

"Definitely," Lena stressed, with her eyes glued to her mother's center.

Not only was Lena ashamed of what happened, but she

prayed that nobody would ever find out. She wondered if her mother was trying to keep her quiet by making her feel guilty. Lena wanted the act to remain hidden and would agree to anything if her mother would really allow her to keep silent. Instinct told Lena that Crystal's abuse of her was a disgrace, and she preferred to keep knowledge of the disgrace limited to them. Lena was afraid that she had somehow been the cause of Crystal's action toward her. Her guilty mind pictured her father seeing the welts on her aching bottom and teasing her about it.

"You don't have to keep our little secret only between us if you don't want to," Crystal said suddenly.

"I want to though, Mommy," Lena mumbled in a plea. "I don't wanna be made fun of."

"I don't blame you," Crystal said with a complacent tone in her voice.

For the first time since she had been born, her mother was in complete control of her.

Lena rose from the bed and Crystal gazed anxiously at Lena's bottom. Lena brushed delicately at her lacerated flesh, where the stinging and heat lingered. She crept quietly to Crystal and smiled sadly, with a deep begging on her face.

"You're not going to tell Daddy, are you?" Lena asked.

"Far as I'm concerned it never happened," Crystal assured Lena with obvious delight.

"Good," Lena was relieved.

"Lena, our little secret is nobody's business but ours," Crystal's tone was tremendously relieving to Lena's ears.

"Mommy, that's exactly the way I feel," Lena explained. "If anybody found out it might make me cry."

Shame was firmly planted in her now, and she agreed to an oath of silence about a disgrace that tormented her and would probably always torment her.

Lena felt that being disgraced by her mother was a sin,

but having that disgrace revealed to her father would be a disaster. She failed to get her mind off of Crystal's bad thing, as she pulled on her panties. Her buttocks felt like they were on fire.

Crystal pushed back Lena's hair and kissed her on the head so sweetly Lena was shocked.

"I turned you back into a good girl, Angel," she said and winked triumphantly. "I knew there was still hope for you."

Crystal picked up the wooden paddle and rubbed it across Lena's buttocks in a threatening way as she went about her business.

Chapter Twelve

Midnight signaled its arrival with twelve chimes of the granddaddy clock and Lena was wading in a sea of torment, recounting each step of how her mother had beaten her with the paddle. Her mind was grieved, devastated; her torment had elevated to such a devastating level that she kept reliving the beating; a tinge of evil seemed to drip from her mother's pores. Why had her mother beaten her senselessly? What had impelled her mother to beat her like that? Had her mother beat her out of hate? Or was there an ulterior motive? And what made her mother take an interest in touching her? Then, as the images played brightly in her mind, she heard footsteps brushing against carpet and her father stepped inside her bedroom.

"Is Daddy's baby asleep?" her father whispered and sat beside her.

Staring and foreboding, Lena avoided her father deliberately. Lena wanted his help, but she could not ask for it and could not accept it, because she did not know how. She was helpless to help herself and felt that even as he offered his help she could not confide in him. The dreadful physical attack leveled against her had left her confused and had washed away her emotional stability, like a tortuous, raging river eroding its banks. Her guilt ridden mind was disturbed because she felt that Crystal may have already told her father about the beating and her father was very disappointed in her for having to be handled like that. I did nothing wrong, she thought angrily, shamefully. She beat me for nothing. Lucky for her that her father was away at work when her mother put her through that physical and emotional torment. Why had her mother beat her so bad?

"When are you going to answer me?" her father asked, with a suspicious tint in his voice.

"I don't know," Lena said as calmly as possible.

"Why not, hon?" her father insisted. "Did Mommy bother you while I was away?"

"Yeah, she did more than bother me. She beat me bad...with a paddle uncle George gave her," Lena admitted painfully.

"With a paddle that Uncle George gave her?" her father said, getting angry, thinking of vengeance against Uncle George. His fingers flicked on the light switch.

She shielded her eyes from the glare. Deep down Lena thought she knew why her mother had abused her. Coupling with her mother's compulsion to be abusive, she knew her mother hated her father and her father hated her mother and that was a reason to beat her so she could strike at her father. That was a common practice among cowards, to strike at someone when they had their back turned and the coward could get away with it. Lena thought at first that she had somehow been at fault for the beating, but the culmination of events was showing her otherwise. The pain in her from the abuse at the hands of her mother had driven a wedge between her and her father and that was exactly what her mother wanted. She could sense it and feel it but could not say it. She knew her father was waiting for a response.

"Just kidding, Dadee," she finally said.

"Huh, uh, I don't think you are," her father spoke in a

passive tone, hoping not to force words into her mouth.

"What?" Lena pretended ignorance, but she realized that she was not duping her father.

She envisioned her body bent over the bed and Crystal whacking her naked buttocks with that paddle, but that did not hurt as much as having her Mommy touching her.

"Don't what to me," her father joked.

"Awright," she answered.

"Did Mommy beat you with Uncle George's paddle?" he asked bluntly.

"No, she just threatened me with it," Lena held to her defense. Her guilty mind fought against letting out the shameful truth.

"You don't have to lie to me," her father said tenderly.

"Please, Dadee, leave me alone?" Lena begged pitifully.

Her father studied her intently, then explained in a heavily concerned voice.

"If you don't tell me the truth you're only hurting yourself."

"Yeah, she beat me," Lena finally confessed. Tears fell from her eyes. "But nothing else."

Lena's last words caused her father to feel sick at his stomach and look at her intently as if studying the meaning of her words.

"That had better be all she done," her father said with anger and blinked his eyes. "That's the typical story that all abused children use. They lie from a combination of fear and guilt and shame. They're afraid that if they speak the truth they'll be abused again in reprisal. The poor innocent kids don't know that it's more dangerous to them if they don't speak. Now, what else happened, Lena?"

"Nothing else happened," Lena cried.

"Don't forget that lying to Daddy is only hurting you," he reminded her.

"I know, Dadee," Lena's voice was still defensive.

"I know you're holding back on me, and I don't think it's bad," his tone was child-like, "but just to make sure I'll ask Mommy."

"Stop it," Lena cried in muffled hysteria. "Leave her out of my life," she urged, recalling her mother touching her bad thing. "I'm not keeping anything from you. So just leave me alone. Please, Dadee!"

The topic was an emotional strain on her, and she was relieved when he softened his approach. He patted her on the head and embraced her firmly, then he let her go.

"Whatever happened will happen again," he said sincerely and smiled softly. "You better tell me while you have a chance, hon."

"Nothing else happened," Lena was resolute in lying to her father. She whimpered, drenched in shame.

"Well, if you're telling the truth, then we ain't got nothing to worry about," her father said after a moment of hesitation. Concern flashed vividly in his brown eyes. We'll just leave it at that."

"Okay," Lena relaxed.

"Good night. I'll see you in the morning," her father said and doused the light.

A distant chime from the ticktock clock signaled that it was one in the morning. Lena could still hear Crystal ordering her to bend over the bed, could feel that paddle smacking her naked flesh, remembered falling into the black pit, heard clearly Crystal telling her to relax as she touched Lena and her bad thing. And she wished she could just blot it all out of her mind. She also wished, with a spark of hope, that if she just forgot about it would her mother just forget about it; if so, she could go back to living a normal life with a normal mother like most kids her age.

Mommy will stop hurting me, she tried to convince herself with her scared, lonely thoughts. She put her face to the wall, welcoming sleep, repelling dread, and was praying her mother would be as loving as she sometimes acted. She failed to defeat the invading tide of guilt and shame that preyed on her mind; she held little respect for her abusive mother who seemed to enjoy tormenting her, and controlling her with fear and violence. She was afraid that possibly her father might vanish if he and her mother continued to fight and then she would be a fatherless child with her abusive mother and that thought gave her symptoms of a bleak future. She would be all alone and helpless. She got a bad taste in her mouth just thinking about it. The thought of her and her mother living all alone made her feel it was impossible to survive her mother's abuse.

A frantic scratching sounded close to her. She jumped up and saw the dark outline of a rat scuttle off her bed.

It was shortly after the ticktock clock chimed two when she finally started shedding tension, her troubled mind relaxing. She was staring at the ceiling in relative comfort, but her guilt was still present, churning profusely. How could she get her mother under her control? Probably by reciprocating the misery. If her father could see exactly what took place after he left the house, he definitely would never have allowed her mother to abuse her again, yet, she also feared that if her father found out the truth he may confront her mother with grave consequences. Neither did she want her mother hurt nor did she want her father to leave. All she wanted was to live in harmony in a happy family. She wanted to extract some form of an understanding from her mother to end the abuse. What kind of understanding could she extract, and would an understanding put this terrifying matter behind them? Maybe a child calling for a truce with a grownup was possible. She tossed and turned for the rest of the night and kept seeing colorful images dancing before her eyes.

At seven sharp her father brought her a breakfast in bed of scrambled eggs emitting a delicious buttery aroma, a piece of cooked ham on a slice of Holsum wheat bread, and a lot of kisses and happiness.

"I could tell what you wanted to eat this morning," her father smiled in emanating delight. "I added milk to the eggs so they'd be fluffy. Taste good?"

"Uh, huh. It's delicious, Dadee."

"Good. Relax and enjoy," her father said so happily it could be heard in his voice. "I just love to take care of my baby."

After she had eaten, her father inspected the lacerations covering her buttocks. Then, he ran his fingers gently across her scalp, feeling for lumps.

"Dadee," she spoke with fear, "where's Mommy?"

Her father smiled, his eyelids flicking with anger.

"Sleeping," he understood Lena's concern. "I know if Mommy sees me checking you she'll be mad, but that only concerns me and her. If she gets out of hand I'll break that paddle over her head."

The shame created by the abuse now felt like a lingering force that would always be there to torment her. She knew she could not repel it so she did not try to.

"Mommy's not my best friend no more," Lena mumbled softly, quietly, careful not to let her mother hear her.

"I wouldn't want a friend that beat me with a paddle either," he replied in support of Lena.

Lena did not reply to her father, nor did she condemn Crystal further. She was surprisingly relieved by confessing her true feelings, but she could sense that there could be even more pain awaiting her. She wished she could live in a home where she would be safe, where nobody would know her as a child who had been abused, a child who had never been stricken with hurt. She felt she could no longer trust her heartless mother and her happy life was gone.

Will I ever be happy again? she wondered.

She accepted her abuse now, could see it as it really was and not how she wanted it to be. When someone came to abuse her, she would know what abuse was, since she had experienced abuse at the hands of her mother. She had no optimism or happiness in her, just a vision of gloom. She had been robbed of her happiness and knew that she may never regain it from a thief of a mother, so she now braced herself determinedly to defy anyone who would try to hurt her. Reality loomed in her life like a palpable mist; she could sense the approach of an endless stream of hardships and she wondered how she would conquer them as they presented themselves. This was the way life was probably meant to be and she readily accepted it. Her thinking became lost in her head as she noticed her father was watching her.

"You must be thinking about something," he said.

"No, not really. Just waiting for you to stop rubbing my head."

"All through." Then after he kissed her cheek he put both hands to her face and stared dead into her eyes. "Lena, I have to tell you the truth if it hurts you or not. Your mother started acting funny when she was four months pregnant with you, and has gotten worse ever since." He stared at her with sadness in his eyes. "A lot of women seem to lose their mind when they give birth. I tried to help her but she wouldn't help herself by letting me help her. Then her mother stepped in and made things worse. She drenched Crystal in pity and Crystal ate it up like a ravenous dog lapping up gravy. She's proudly following in the footsteps of her mother without realizing its implications."

Lena nodded, her cesspool life just absorbed more sewage. She appreciated her father's concern, but his words rattled her brain almost as bad as her mother had rattled it. She could not handle hearing more information on her mother, and she could not handle more of her mother's abuse. She was facing a dilemma she could not solve and now she was more confused. She did realize her father was trying to help her by informing her of the development of her mother's behavior.

Her life had become a living nightmare that showed no signs of relenting; and there was no escape in sight. The image of her mother touching her had gradually fizzled away; she was tucking it away into the deepest part of her mind where she would not have to see it all the time. She did not want to remember it had ever happened; it was too shameful and disgraceful.

She sat down, happy that she had her father with her. She felt she was innocent. So what did she do wrong...why did she beat her so bad? I can't stop her, she thought and filled with an angry sadness. I didn't deserve to be beaten unconscious....

She felt weak and sick and lay down on her bed. Her father sat beside her. Disgusted with her guilt, the abuse, her life, she could only dream of peace.

She imagined her life wrapped in happiness, genuine soothing happiness, overwhelming the anxiety bubbling in her. She had been feeling nauseous and the urge to vomit had subsided as she relaxed and sipped green Gatorade. She was happy that her mind was rapidly adjusting to her wonderful home life.

Chapter Thirteen

North of Broward Boulevard on State Road Seven she saw that the Health and Rehabilitative Services Department was set back from the highway. The parking lot was full and big beat up Buicks and Cadillacs were parked alongside polished Camrys and Mercedes with gold plated bumpers and gleaming wire rims costing hundreds of dollars. Most of the occupants of the cars had bumper stickers proclaiming Black Power and Puerto Rican Power, and they were coming in for their monthly supply of food stamps that they would sell to a grocery store for thirty percent to purchase alcohol, drugs, tobacco products, and, if enough was left, maybe make a car payment.

The well structured HRS building looked like a bustling sea of poverty, misery and misfortune. She unsnapped her safety belt as Jim parked the car in the run down parking lot spotted with mud puddles, beer cans and decaying cigarette butts, a hint of worry showing in his movements. Lena was nervous, feeling a cold lump of dread lying in her stomach. She got out of the car with her father and stood under the heat of a pitiless sun.

"Lena," her father said, kneeling beside her. "We got to go inside and talk with somebody about Mommy...."

"Awright, Dadee," she made herself look calm.

EYES OF A CHILD 111

"Are you scared, Lena?" he asked, smiling down at her. "It won't take but a few minutes."

"I've been thinking about things," Lena said quietly, forming a vivid picture of the paddle and her mother's bad thing.

"Well, just stop thinking so much," he encouraged. "All thinking does is make you worry. And your Daddy doesn't want that."

"Thanks," Lena said. She held her eyes on the entrance of the building where the bold dark letters HRS were situated above two thin and six thick white stucco support columns whose bases were tarnished with dirt.

"You don't have to thank me." Her father quickly explained, smiling welcomely. "I know you have always appreciated me."

"I do, Dadee," she assented, fighting anxiety.

"Listen, Lena, after all this is over your mother will be nice to you," he promised her with all the strength in his tone, petting her head to restore her confidence. "Reporting her to the authorities is the only way to control her." His anxious words were masked in solemn belief. "Lena, I can predict your mother's actions before she acts. She would do anything for my attention, which makes her a threat to your physical well being. Hon, keep your confidence in your Daddy who cares about you and the stars will shine for you. I hope you understand what I'm talking about." He stopped talking, hoping his forceful speech had the impact he wanted it to have on her.

Lena knew that her father was seeking help for her from the authorities and would never give up until he got what he wanted.

"I'll guarantee you that the courts will make a mother out of your mother," he spoke firmly as they passed by the stucco support columns and stood underneath the portico. "But don't get the wrong idea now. I wouldn't hurt your mother for nothing in the world; I'm not that way. If I hurt her I would be hunting you anyway." He forced a false smile bursting with tension. "I promise you, you will be all right, hon."

"I sure hope so," Lena whined uneasily.

"Hon, you got to turn your stumbling blocks into stepping stones and life will always be bright," her father said matter-of-factly.

Lena just listened. She had hoped for a briefing on the benefit of coming here, instead, she was amply showered with goodwill prose and unconfirmed promises that kept her on edge. She felt that what she did not tell her father was what he was worried about. She was worried about herself and she saw that her father was worried about her.

"Both of us are going to solve all our problems today, hon." Her father spoke even as they went inside the building through manual doors.

The lobby was decorated and dimmed by tinted plate glass windows and bluish carpeting running halfway up the gray walls and Lena stood nervously before a bleached blond black lady sitting behind window number six. Her black face glares beneath her blond hair, she thought timidly. Her serious blue eyes scare me and they look as cautious and mournful as a cat's. Lena felt an urge to tell her father how the lady looked to her. Then she decided against it. It was not important or polite.

Straight ahead of Lena were windows one through eight and doors A through C. The lobby looked shabby and dingy and the faded blue tile and the couch-like rows of blue vinyl chairs with rips and cigarette burns made things worse. Everybody she saw looked beaten and defeated and even the well dressed case workers seemed to have that same beater-in-life look.

Her father had been watching her sizing up the place.

"There is nothing to worry about, Lena. You can put all your bad days behind you; your father is the only friend you will probably ever have in your entire life. Everybody else that comes in your life are just acquaintances. Your mother is also supposed to be a true friend, but she has proven to be your true enemy. Take a seat now and I'll be right back, hon," her father said and patted her on the head again.

Lena stared worriedly after her father; she wanted to stop him and tell him to take her back home, but her logic was too lame to alter her father's decision to seek legal recourse.

"Dadee, what's going to happen?" she asked sheepishly, expecting her ears to absorb his worst answer.

"Nothing that's going to hurt you," her father was blunt.

"Are you sure?" Lena asked as the lump of dread in her stomach broke up into churning bits of stone.

"I'm surer than sure."

"Awright," Lena said. She folded her hands together, hoping to give the impression of being relaxed. "I'll wait right here for you."

Lena watched her father talk to the blond-haired black lady sitting behind window number six. Gradually, her tension eased and she loosened the grip on her fingers and she started to feel normal again. A minute later her father returned and sat next to her. Again he was smiling, as if to assure her that his smile meant that everything was going to be all right. She knew she would keep the dread that she was feeling locked in her mind. Out of Door A, a smiling, attractive, slender lady suddenly appeared and beckoned them inside.

"Do come in please, please," the lady said.

"Let's go," her father said, holding her by the hand.

After Lena settled herself in her office she had a uncomfortable feeling that the lady could read her mind, could detect her dread, the tormenting dread that lived inside her.

"I'm Mrs. Linda Rosenblum," she introduced herself.

"The one you spoke to over the phone."

"Nice to meet you," her father said. "I'm Jim Smith as you know."

Mrs. Rosenblum looked at Lena with placating eyes.

"So this is the lovely little lady you told me about." Her gentle smiling slightly allayed Lena's foreboding. "She's every bit the doll you said she was."

"I don't lie."

"No, I don't think you do ," she told her father. "You think she will talk to me?"

"I don't see why not. She talked to me."

"But you're not a stranger to her like I am," she explained. "Anyway, Jim, let me explain a few things to you before I speak with Lena. Female abusers are rare, especially sexual abusers. But that doesn't mean your wife is innocent. If the female abuses, she usually abuses female children even if a male child is available. Child abuse is basically a male sickness. Child abuse has known to exist throughout time and in every social strata. Believe it or not, sometimes it has been given sanction by traditional and ritual usage; more often, it has been a matter of private acts committed in shameful secrecy." She put her hands slowly in her pockets as though she was steadying herself to endure this dreaded subject. "For instance, society these days say that even mentally deranged people are entitled to do exactly what they want with their kids and action can only be taken against them when they have broken the law.

"How does society determine that the law has been broken?"

She blinked her eyes sadly and put her hands to her face. "When there has been severe injury or death of the child. It's a shame and society knows it. See, society sometimes has viewed children as chattels, humans without rights of their own. It's wrong, but tell society that.

"Some cultures have a very low incidence of abuse, but in other cultures the incidence is high and it is extremely high in so called Western society. Western society at times has identified strongly with the child abuser and, like the abuser, they show little respect for human life." Mrs. Rosenblum winked at Lena and smiled. "I'll be right with you, sweetheart.

"If the end result is not death for the child, then regardless of how severe or minor the abuse is, severe psychological damage causing permanent defects in development and in personality occur.

"Family life for the abused child is distorted and filled with violence, shouting, misery, disorganization, and lack of comfort, understanding and encouragement, or quiet and cold and negative with or without outbursts of violence. Yes, to them this is normal even though it is abnormal. The abused child usually raises his or her family in the same manner under which they were raised, thus perpetuating the vicious cycle of abuse. If the abused female does not abuse her children, she is usually the mother of victims. It's so sad, isn't it, Jim?"

Jim nodded. Lena was trembling, thinking dreamily of being shuffled from one abusive monster to another. She blinked her eyes wonderingly. Was her mother really crazy and what did crazy really mean? Was it similar to when a woman who was married for thirty years suddenly loses her husband and then she starts doing odd things and acting in strange ways, like beating her daughter and flaunting her bad thing? Well, if that was it then her mother was really crazy.

"Well, let's see if she's going to talk to me," she said, smiling as she took her hands away from her face.

Mrs. Rosenblum sat, turned in her chair and pulled a book off the shelf, then set it in front of her and smiled at Lena.

"Lena, when people have no respect for themselves they don't respect others," she stressed. "You may not understand my philosophy but with time you will. Your father said that you have something important to tell me, is that so?"

"No," Lena flatly replied. "Not that I know of."

"Take it easy, Lena," Jim interrupted. "You're overly upset because you're probably confused." Jim blinked rapidly. "Look, Mrs. Rosenblum is here to help. She's my counselor, and yours too. Now go ahead and tell her how Mommy beat you and I'll tell her the rest."

"No, Dadee," Lena protested. She twisted and whispered in Jim's ear. "I'm too scared."

A sad look showed on Jim's face. He kissed her then tightened his fists.

"Lena, If you don't talk to her you're only making the situation worse." He sounded angry. "There's no other way for you to get help? She's got to hear you tell her about your mother, understand?"

"What did she say, Jim?" Mrs. Rosenblum asked eagerly.

Jim patted Lena's thigh reassuringly and mumbled in a cold deadly tone.

"She said she's scared. It just kills me."

"Sure it does, but it won't solve nothing," she assured.

"Why doesn't she just tell you of her abuse?" Jim asked.

"Because she's scared. You heard what she said," Mrs. Rosenblum said. "There are many reasons why abused children won't talk. Fear of further abuse; loyalty to the family; feeling that they deserved it; being overwhelmed by the assault. The child may not feel able to trust an adult. Or he or she may feel that assaults from adult to child are part of existence, as indeed they are in some families. The child may have to be removed from the abusive environment, and when the child can feel itself in a caring and safe environment, then he or she may begin to talk to a trusted adult about what happened. We have to just keep trying. Sooner or later she'll talk, they always do, Jim."

"But I ain't patient," Jim grumbled under his breath. He angrily turned to his daughter. "Lena, make a decision, talk to Mrs. Rosenblum or handle it all alone." Jim could not have been more blunt.

"It's all in your hands now."

Lena felt a deep shock. Her father had suggested of backing out, if she did not obey him, and abandon his effort to help her. He had drawn the line of his coaxing her to talk and the effectiveness of his authority over her.

"Are you saying I have to tell her everything or else you won't help me no more?"

"That's exactly it," he said, his anger subsiding. "Now talk."

With drawn face, Lena mentioned the whipping she had gotten, the wooden paddle, the pain, the anger, but when she thought of her mother's bad thing, she stuttered, trembled, and passed it up; she just wanted to forget about that part; and she refused to mention her terrifying fall into the bottomless black pit of unconsciousness. She refused to mention the shame she felt; she strongly felt that no one would ever believe her, because she did not believe it herself. And definitely, she could never mention the guilt that now was part of her. And, now, she could not feel any reality of her mother touching her.

She shrugged her shoulders in a pitiful gesture that showed she was done and hoped she would not get caught lying.

Mrs. Rosenblum put the book upright on her lap and crossed her legs and scoffed.

"Come on, Jim, you seem to be wasting my valuable time and yours too. You have nothing against your wife. Child abuse is the killing, maiming, starving, neglect, cruel punishment and sexual exploitation of children. So she spanked Lena a little harder than usual, but that's not abuse. Abuse should have been self explanatory to you. Abuse." She stressed the term pensively enough to make him think. "Something out of the ordinary has to happen. Like breaking her arm, fracturing her skull, pedophilia or neglecting her to where her life is in danger. Besides, Jim, signs of physical abuse usually show injuries to the face, mouth and head. Children who have been killed or severely injured have had injuries particularly to those areas. Their injuries often occur with multiple bruises, like an injury from a fist with a ring on it. Multiple scars of different ages may be seen on the face, head or elsewhere. I see no injuries on her exterior, nor are there any scars. Your child apparently has not suffered any of these abuses, Jim. What I would like to elaborate on is your belief that her mother deliberately poured scalding coffee on your daughter's chest. Now, first, let's see the lacerations you told me about?"

"Sure," Jim snapped. "I see my interpretation of child abuse was wrong." He was getting the feeling that she was siding with Lena's mother and he was about to ask for a different counselor.

"No, Dadee," Lena whined.

"Mrs. Rosenblum is only going to take a fast look, hon," Jim was blunt. He took down Lena's pants.

Mrs. Rosenblum put on her glasses and looked closely at the fading marks on Lena's bottom. Then she stared at Jim.

"I've seen worse," Mrs. Rosenblum said, pulling off her glasses, "and that wasn't abuse."

"Look how small she is though," Jim argued irritably, almost losing his temper. "She can't take beatings like that."

"Relax, you're overreacting," Mrs. Rosenblum accused softly. "If she had cigarette burns or dunking scalds from boiling water on her buttocks, that would be reason for alarm. But thank God she doesn't. Anyways, let's see the scar on her chest." She tilted her head, as though she was overly concerned.

As her father pulled off her red polo shirt, she suddenly

saw her bedroom with her mother, that paddle smacking her bare flesh, that bottomless pit of blackness swallowing her, her Mommy's bad thing that had aroused more terror in her, and she knew that she was helpless with her father who was helpless to prevent her from being abused again. She jumped up and threw a crying tantrum.

"What's wrong with you, Lena?" Jim beseeched. A look of understanding came to his eyes. "I got it. Our talking has upset you, hasn't it? Jim kissed his daughter on both cheeks, pampering her profusely. "Don't be sad! There's nothing to worry about."

"There's plenty to worry about," Mrs. Rosenblum tried to explain.

"Not when I'm with her!" Jim was up in hostility.

At last Lena accepted how brutal her world was, she had also accepted that her father was powerless. As her tantrum raged, she realized that she was compelled to weep, so she wept for herself, for her father's anguish and concern, for the anger he screened with forced smiles. She felt with a deep sense that nobody would ever be able to help her. Because nobody was any good. Everybody was bad like her mother.

And she was no longer shocked that the world was full of child abusers, molesters, and mean mothers who thrived on pulling out little girl's hair.

"That's all it is," Jim pacified, kissing his daughter again. "You're upset that's all. But don't worry. You'll learn to live with it sooner or later."

Jim fixed his hurt eyes on Mrs. Rosenblum's eyes, then exposed the shrinking scar on Lena's chest.

"It's almost gone now, so it's not much to concern ourselves with," Jim informed with mild sarcasm.

Mrs. Rosenblum gaped and her glasses almost fell off.

"Good God, Jim. Stop trying to be sarcastic. That scar is downright horrible."

"Not really. It's getting smaller everyday."

"Stop it, Jim," Mrs. Rosenblum scolded with a deep moan.

Mrs. Rosenblum analyzed the scar then stared into Lena's tear streaked face and her eyes dripped tears.

"That scalding coffee must have burned her to her bones," she complained loudly.

"No, not that far," Jim offered with more sarcasm, happy that Mrs. Rosenblum was angrily concerned now.

"This is no joking matter, Jim," Mrs. Rosenblum advised. "If that burn was non accidental, she must be a lunatic, a pathological child abuser. How could anybody do that? So you're sure your wife deliberately poured the coffee on Lena?"

"I know she did, but I can't prove it because I didn't see her," Jim explained. "Nobody saw her. Lena and Crystal were alone in the kitchen and suddenly I heard my Lena let out a horrible scream. I ran in and seen my poor baby clenching her chest and laboring to draw in some air so she could scream again. Her face was contorted with an agony of the dying. God, her skin just peeled off from the scorching coffee; it took off her nipples too. Second degree burns is what Dr. Ehrlich said they were."

Lena wept again, feeling confused at the subject. Her father assumed she was weeping only since she was upset, but she was weeping for her feeling of helplessness, for her father who was powerless.

"I feel like killing that bitch!" her father spoke angrily. "She's hurt you, my daughter!" He wiped Lena's teary face and stroked her hair. "I should go home and kill her now, hack her up with an ax."

Lena stopped her crying and lashed at him. "Sure you could! But you won't!"

Jim's throat constricted, then he breathed deeply, smiling pleasingly at Lena's words.

"Did I hear you right, Lena? It's too good to believe." Did she really want him to take care of her mother? He was full of joy now.

"You're helpless, Dadee! And I'm helpless too. That's right, I said then why don't you?"

"Jim," Mrs. Rosenblum interrupted. "Stop, it's too much on her."

Jim's eye twitched. He paled and trembled weakly on his feet, then smiled and studied Mrs. Rosenblum's expression, his mood deadly.

"You hear her...she wants me to relieve her of her mother."

"How can you blame her?" Mrs. Rosenblum said. "Evil feeds on evil but it doesn't last forever."

The truth of Lena's desire filled her with pity for her mother and she immediately recanted her suddenly truthful feelings. Her mother was a sad image of a mother but at least she had a mother.

"No, Dadee! I want my Mommy," she cried.

Mrs. Rosenblum sat back in her chair, her head quivering as she opened the book and flipped through the pages.

"Even abused children want their mothers, Jim," she said in a voice of profound concern. "Children are overly wanted by their mothers, regardless if they abuse them. In the past it was believed that the opposite was true. See, the mother sometimes has high expectations of her child and when the child fails to meet those expectations the mother becomes agitated and abuses her child. This explains why many child victims still love their mothers who have mutilated them. They know that there is a lot of love for them because at times, they have experienced it. On the other hand, I think we really have something on your wife, Jim."

"It's no surprise to me."

"But I must warn you that the burden of proof is on the

State, and scalds can be very difficult to prove as deliberate," Mrs. Rosenblum said. "See, the direction and area of the splash marks can help determine if the injury was deliberate. In accidental scalds the arms, hands and front of the child is predominantly the area involved, whereas it may not be so in inflicted injuries, but of course, it can be. As you can see Lena's scald is to the front of her which can be argued as being accidental."

"She's burned to the front because that's where her mother decided on the spur of the moment to burn her," Jim told her.

"I want to go home, Dadee," Lena moaned with a teary face. She climbed from her chair and hugged her father's neck. He picked her up delicately.

"Now you just stop your crying, little lady."

"Dadee, I wanna go home to my Mommy."

"Lena, you can't be serious."

Lena relaxed her head on her father's shoulder as he expressed hatred toward her mother. "I know that kids want to go back to the parent who has abused them," Jim complained. "They have nobody else. What a tragedy—"

"They're confused too that's why, Jim. Hey, Jim! Listen:

"Whoever causes or permits any child less than eighteen years of age to suffer, or inflicts upon it unjustifiable physical pain or mental suffering, or willingly causes or permits the life of any such child to be endangered or its health to be injured, or such child to be placed in such situation that its life may be endangered or its health injured....shall be guilty of a felony of the second degree.... Your wife is walking on ice, Jim."

"Great," Jim smiled. "Her past is finally catching up with her. My baby's suffering's coming to an end. My struggle's beginning to pay off. That's good news," Jim was almost ecstatic. "We got her now."

Mrs. Rosenblum turned the page and crossed her legs tighter.

"Quit ranting just for a moment, Jim, and pay attention:

"...Any person convicted of the crime of child abuse shall be imprisoned in a penitentiary for a term of not less than one year and may extend to life...

"How does that sound?"

"Like a million dollars," Jim flaunted his jovial mirth.

"If we can prove that she willfully and deliberately poured hot coffee on your daughter's chest we can lock her up and throw away the key."

"Now that's justice!"

"We have grounds of reasonable suspicion to pull her into court."

"What are we waiting for?"

"I'll have my assistant draw up the charges and get the permission of my superior...I'll have the sheriff serve her notice. Keep all this quiet, Jim. Don't say a word and we'll catch her by surprise. She might get scared and admit everything." Her words offered justified satisfaction. "She'll convict herself in the end. That's the way it usually happens."

"You're right about that, Mrs. Rosenblum," Jim agreed.

Lena was still scared, for she did not believe that her abuse could be coming to an end. Why had her parents created a family based upon hostility, built an intangible relationship based upon nothing? Her gloomy life was turning more into a dreaded dream every time she blinked her eyes.

"If she's convicted I hope she burns," Mrs. Rosenblum said with glassy eyes. "What kind of mother would mistreat her children?"

Jim stopped moving, then sat in a chair. "The lowest type of bastard," he judged.

"I'm compelled to agree with that sentiment," Mrs. Rosenblum confessed. She turned to Lena in a sweet, soothing tone. "How are you doing there?"

"Just fine."

"She's always fine, Mrs. Rosenblum." He looked more

at ease and the tension had left his voice. "She's just had a few bad moments in her life."

"It happens to the best of us, Jim."

"Yeah, you're right." Jim was genuine. "I've seen it happen to the best."

Lena finally felt driven to ignore Mrs. Rosenblum; she seemed unable to be herself before Mrs. Rosenblum's watchful green eyes even though her passive nature had put her somewhat at ease.

"Why would she abuse my baby?" Jim complained. "She's probably ignorant."

"Child abuse has nothing to do with ignorance," Mrs. Rosenblum corrected. "Child abusers are usually intelligent people who have a perverse fascination with punishment, and the cold calculation of destruction which in itself requires neither provocation nor rationale. The one invariable trademark of the child abuser regardless of economic or social status is this immersion in the action of punishing without regard for its cause or its purpose. Better yet, it's called, punishment without crime. Its violence creates terror and panic for the child, but it does not teach the child any rational means of avoiding that violence. And to make it worse it usually strikes without warning, which makes it even more terrifying to the child. A child abuser is a deliberate, calculated, consistent and tortuous animal."

"Then maybe she's crazy," Jim said.

"Now that's possible," Mrs. Rosenblum said. "She very well could be an undiagnosed schizophrenic, and suffers from a delusion that you favor Lena over her."

"You know, Mrs. Rosenblum," Jim said. "Once I was peeking through the window of the house and was watching Crystal ranting and raving at Lena like Lena had been imposed upon her by some wicked force out of a fairy tale. Probably the Wizard of Oz, which levels with her mentality. And

I heard her using phrases like 'your evil like my father; you were born wicked like your father; you're a monster like my mother; you act like an animal like my dog my mother put to sleep,' that's one of the many reasons why I think she's crazy."

"If she acted like that," Mrs. Rosenblum stated, "she's got to be crazy. Jim, most child abusers are unaware that there is anything wrong with their behavior or that others find it reprehensible; to them their behavior is normal. But, of course, these are your low class child abusers, and your wife is definitely low class. The middle class child abusers are very cautious in their behavior. Also the middle class abusers usually do not neglect physical care of their children, not, at least, in ways visible to the outside community. By the way what is an educated man like yourself doing with someone like that anyways? Maybe it's you that's crazy."

"Could be," Jim broke out in laughter along with Mrs. Rosenblum. "I've never claimed to be normal. And I've never claimed to be sane enough to pick out a decent woman to birth my baby."

"Well, Jim, you've made your bed, even if it was unintentional," Mrs. Rosenblum said, "and now you're wallowing in the misery you helped create."

Their eyes met until they both stopped laughing.

"Take your daughter home, Jim," Mrs. Rosenblum said. "She's had a miserable day. Till you hear from me, keep a low profile. Don't offer a hint to your wife that something is going on. Be yourself. Surprise is our best weapon. Even with the last breath in my body, I'll do everything I can to help your poor child."

"Thanks, Mrs. Rosenblum."

"I'm only doing my job."

"Well, I appreciate it."

"Okay, Jim. I'll be in touch. Go on and take Lena home."

"Okay," he agreed, standing with Lena in his arms.

"If anything strange happens, just call me," Mrs. Rosenblum said.

"Thanks again." Jim happily accepted Mrs. Rosenblum's offer.

Back out under the portico, Lena squirmed out of her father's arms.

"I'll walk now, Dadee."

"About time. You're almost too big for me to carry anymore." He squinted sternly at Lena. "You been watching any murder movies?"

"No, Dadee, just cartoons and Frazzle Rock."

"What made you say I wouldn't kill your mother?"

"I was mad, Dadee."

"Lena, I don't ever want to hear you say that again even if you are mad."

"Awright."

"We have to work this problem out together, hon." Her father lectured. "You work with me and I'll work with you. Daddy loves you. I'm here to make you happy and healthy all of your life. Now, I'm taking you somewhere you wanna go."

Lena smiled happily. "To Chuck E. Cheese, Dadee?"

"Nope."

"Then where?"

"It's a surprise."

"Awright."

Chapter Fourteen

Happy, relaxed, she wiped the last tears of dread from her eyes. She had trusted her life with her mother thinking she was safe and it was so funny she could not laugh without having a heart attack. Labeling Crystal a child abuser had enclosed her in a world of confusion and now she had lost all faith in the person she trusted the most. She wanted to cower in a corner or hide her face or crawl under the bed or anything to just get away from ever having to deal with her mother again. Maybe she would lock herself in a closet forever. Or maybe she would go to sleep and never wake up again.

"Let's go, Lena."

"Awright," she said and started for the car.

"Let's walk," her father said, holding her hand.

A blanket of clouds seemed to be brushing the spires of tall buildings.

"Where you taking me, Dadee?"

"Down the street."

"What's down there?"

"A nice place to relax," Jim stressed.

Relaxing on a high seat beside her father in Ronald McDonald's, she devoured McNuggets and fries and honey, quenching her thirst with icy root beer, followed with vanilla ice cream and strawberries and chopped nuts, with a Maraschino cherry on top.

"Taste good?" her father asked with joy in his voice.

"Oh, yeah."

Noon had arrived after they exited McDonald's. Lena clung close to her father with a stuffed tummy, her eyes heavy with weariness and in need of a nap.

"I'm so full, Dadee."

"Yeah. I know," he said as heavy traffic rumbled past. He offered to carry her but she refused.

When they reached the car a brutal yellow sun broke through thick clouds. On the opposite side of the street was Castle Park decorated with colorful statues, blooming flowers, a miniature golf course, with silver ponds beneath wooden bridges, slender pines and luscious shrubbery.

"Hon, isn't Castle Park a beautiful sight? It's open for anyone who wants to enjoy themselves. You can see that there are only a few people there lounging. For some reason not many people are there. I would say that most people stay away because they don't like enjoyment, pleasure, the finer things in life. See, what I'm driving at is that evidently your poor blind mother would rather induce pain and misery and hardship for herself and her family instead of happiness. Your mother's not fully accountable for her erratic nature. See, your grandmother was a blind old widow who was lonely and miserable throughout her life. She felt no meaning to her existence, so she gave your mother a life filled with abuse, and, by doing this, your mother lived a miserable life. Your grandmother then had meaning in her life.

"I know I'm speaking over your head but just listen anyway. Your mother then grew up without any meaning to her life. So, in return, your mother gives you the same life that her mother gave her. Now your mother too has a meaning to her existence, a horribly negative existence but an existence. Just like a chain reaction. You're not going to be like that because I'm not going to let it happen. I'm going to help you by cracking a link in that chain. I hope you grow up to be educated, hon. More educated than me. I'm behind you. I've already paid for your education by enrolling you in the Florida Prepaid College Program. For a girl coming out of poverty, you're lucky and you don't know it. As of now, I hope you understand that some people like hardships, and others don't. I want you to be one that doesn't.

"I ain't trying to make you dislike your mother, but only to understand her. What I'm doing here is for your safety, not hostility toward your mother. Any problems you have, just let me know. I eventually want to see you as the happiest person in the world. Lena that's everything: happiness. How you feel is extremely important; a good self image is extremely important; if you're not happy you probably won't have a good image of yourself. And if you feel down, you're defeated without even knowing it. If you are happy you're on top of the world and it improves your chances of success. If I keep pounding this into your mind you will eventually understand, hon." Jim's lecture was strong, and imploring.

"I heard what you said, Dadee," she crackled humbly, feeling too tired to talk anymore.

"Lena, I know you heard me. I'm going to infuse you with insight, so you can avoid the grief your mother couldn't avoid."

She blinked and stared at her father. Insight? What was insight? A tide of confusion drenched her, but she held back her urge to question him. How did insight relate to child abuse, guilt and shame? Well, she was too tired to ask him; maybe someday she would ask.

"You being mistreated by your mother is going to end," her father explained angrily. Loudly he fell into more explaining. "Your mother is good, but she's a little disturbed I think. She's allowing her emotions to think for her and it's harming you. I'll be helping her by helping you through the courts." He kissed her then pet her on the head. "I'm sorry if I've bothered you. I'll stop if you want me to. I just felt that I should explain this to you."

Drowsy, struggling to keep her mind on her father, she could hardly believe that the time for her to learn about her mother had arrived when she had least wanted to hear about it. She was locked in thought.

Her father was concerned for her. She knew that she would never learn otherwise. His actions spoke for themselves. She listened to his lecture, understanding almost everything, revering his knowledge, his logic. Her father was unleashing all the chronic problems of her mother's life, revealing all the true, pitiful facts. She glimpsed vaporous heat twisting on the streets, repelled the smothering humidity, and she was revived, with doubt and happiness, upon a distant hope of a better life. She had ardently daydreamed about subduing her mother, nullifying her abuse, and both her and her mother appreciating each other; but now she was being confronted with a fantasy that, realistically, could never happen. I would jump at the first chance to conquer her, she thought.

Through tired eyes, she saw a strange man smile and wink.

She was not at all surprised that her father seemed to know everything in life.

"Lena," Jim said tenderly, affectionately, "what I've been telling you about should he kept a secret. It's what a concerned father tells his abused daughter."

"Awright," she mumbled in assent.

"See, when we get home, I want you to act natural," her father urged, sniffing disgustedly at the thickening traffic's polluting fumes. "I know it'll he hard to do, hon, but you can do it for our sake. Listen, Lena, nobody, other than Mrs. Rosenblum and my attorney, Scott Armstrong, knows about today; he will be with us in court to see that we get a fair fight against your mother. So try not to accidentally mention something that may alert your mother."

Lena blinked happily with rounded eyes. How blind she was. Her father had to tell her how to handle her mother when she already thought she knew how. Her father whom she loved lived his life for her, and someday, she too, would be equally learned. Her father was more knowledgeable than she had ever realized. That was why he had always lectured her.

"Dadee, thanks."

"Don't mention it, Lena," Jim said politely. "It's my duty. If you follow me you'll be okay. You should understand that I'm here to help you, protect you."

"That's so nice of you, Dadee."

"Well, thank you, hon. You'll soon learn that problems with your mother are problems that can be remedied so don't worry yourself to death about them. When you've experienced problems early in life you've built up experience for them later in life. That's why you can't let them get the best of you. Problems are just a way of life in some families. I didn't have a close family when I was growing up because my mother broke it up. I wanted a close family with you but your mother is trying to break it up. I've learned to live with it and I want you to learn to live with it.

"Good times never last forever and bad times never last forever. I experienced problems as a kid and I've experienced them as an adult and I overcame them all. And I didn't make an issue out of them because I didn't want to, and that's smart. Lena, tolerate life as it presents itself. You can't run or hide from them because they are a part of you. Look at every problem in life as a learning experience. After the years pass you will look back on them and realize how much you learned. Nothing can defeat you unless you let it."

Jim inserted the car key into the door and unlocked it.

"We're going to go home, Lena," Jim promised her.

"I'm so tired," Lena said in haste.

"I bet," Jim said. "I would be tired too."

She climbed across the driver's seat of the car and he slid in behind her and cranked the engine.

"Fight anything that bothers you, hon," her father urged.

"Okay, Dadee," Lena said, straining to keep her eyes open.

After fastening her safety belt she leaned her head on the door handle and fell asleep. She awoke on the living room couch.

Reality was unveiling itself. She had reentered her troubled environment. She was back in her rat infested shack, and she, Lena, could be stuck forever in this horrible position, could lead a life similar to her mother and have a lifetime of misery. Her father gave her an understanding of tolerance and optimism to deal with the matter. This made her feel as if he had given her the world. She tilted her head and was surprised to see her mother standing by her.

"You slept for an hour," Crystal said with a soft smile. "Where have y'all been, Angel?"

"Eating lunch," Lena said in a whining tune.

"Yeah, that's what your father said," Crystal said strangely, placing her hands on her hips and trying to read Lena.

Lena blinked tiredly and yawned deeply. Peace and pleasure had seized the moment. There was not any bickering or contention. It looked like a united family in perfect harmony. Then Crystal was suspiciously analyzing her with an unwavering stare; Lena closed her eyes and hoped, hoping to stop more questioning. Jim was in a trance watching a boxing match on cable television.

"I was waiting for you and your father to get home to have lunch with me," Crystal said, trying to make Lena feel bad by sounding sad. "I guess I just have to eat all by myself."

"Huh?"

Lena was trying to ignore her mother. "You talking to me, Mommy?"

Crystal glared down at Lena.

"Not to anyone, but you," she said abruptly. "And don't play stupid with me."

Words of hysteria suddenly erupted from Jim.

"It's all over! Mike Tyson just knocked out Trevor Berbick for a second time. He's still the undisputed WBA heavyweight champion of the world! Berbick put up a great fight though. It would have been nice to see Berbick bring the title back to Coach Kenny's gym where I work out at since Coach Chico's gym closed down."

"Who has the title, Dadee?"

"Mike Tyson, hon."

"But how come?"

"Because he's the best fighter in the world today."

As he slipped a tape that he had filmed in the VCR his face flashed on the screen with Coach Angelo in the ring training him. In the background Coach Chico and Norman were both sitting, appearing listless and lazy as Angelo trained everybody. But they were not lazy; they were businessmen and only trained for money. Coach Angelo showed Dr. Seminelli how to bob and weave. Angelo is the only one giving away anything free, Norman said. Chico nodded in accord with Norman. Then Jim ejected the tape.

Crystal groaned. She said the topic of boxing agitated her, and she left.

Lena was happy to see her leave the living room. She stretched her limbs like a cat and lay back down. Most of her built up tension, aching anxiety, fear, and anger vanished and she was soothingly secure for the moment and she wished that this peace would never leave. She was lucky to have such a concerned father and now would turn to nobody but him. As she closed her eyes in peace and quiet, there came a moment of happiness, a flitter of stars in her mind, a vague anxiousness that induced a rush of pleasant emotions that she never believed existed.

As she relaxed, her father picked her up gently and delicately and gave her a big, pacifying hug of kindness.

"Lena," Jim's voice was deeply emotional.

"Yes, Dadee?"

"Hon, you dealt with it like an adult. You're stronger than what I ever expected. You've stunned your Daddy and made him proud too."

"What do you mean, Dadee?"

"When we saw Mrs. Rosenblum you were strong, real strong."

"Sure, but I had you with me."

"That doesn't mean nothing," he said. He kissed her on the cheek. "Either you're strong or you're not. Lena?"

"Huh, Dadee?"

"You're not scared about going to court with your mother there, are you? I know it creates a lot of guilt and shame for a child to go against a parent, especially by the encouragement of another parent."

"I'm a little scared, Dadee."

"Why?"

"I don't know. I just am."

"You think she might beat you for it when I'm not around? That's got to be it," he said, his face feeling hot. "But don't worry, hon. She won't mistreat you again."

Lena smiled in happiness.

"You really think so, Dadee?"

"Lena, I know so," her father said flatly, his eyelids trembling anxiously. "Just watch and see." His eyes darted about.

"Her days of child abuse have come to an end. And I think she knows it." He smiled, touching the mist sparkling on her face. "If the law doesn't stop her, I will. Lena, after you grow up, you will realize with sadness that it's a tragedy when your own flesh and blood mistreats you."

"I'd rather forget it by then."

"Well, you probably will. But in your subconscious you will somehow know that your mother tried to hurt you, ruin you, bring you to her level, when you were a child." Jim smiled again. "I'll help you to forget the dark days of your life," he promised.

Lena was drenched in happiness.

"Uh, oh, thank you...Uh, I'm so glad."

"Relax," Jim coaxed. "Hon, there's no reason to stutter. Just slow down. Your worst days are over, I promise, just trust me."

"Awright, Dadee," she promised.

"So you will keep faith in me?" Jim asked.

"I sure will."

She was staring back into his eyes in the quiet of the house. Jim held Lena's body like he never wanted to turn her loose.

"Are you still as scared of your mother as before?" Jim questioned with hope.

"Dadee, I don't understand you."

"You should understand me, Lena."

"I should, Dadee?"

"Sure you should. Since we talked to Mrs. Rosenblum you shouldn't be as scared of your mother anymore." His words reflected endless concern.

Lena was sad for her father, more than she was for herself. He had wanted her to feel secure so bad that he insisted that their visit to Mrs. Rosenblum had relieved her of the fear that Crystal had instilled in her. She knew that she had not been thoroughly relieved of the fear she was feeling.

"Well, maybe you still are as scared," Jim said heartily.

"Yes, I am, Dadee." She was truthful because she did not want to be a liar like her mother.

"Well," Jim moaned. "That was not what I wanted to hear. But at least you're truthful. I just don't want you living in fear. Lena, this is not the Dark Ages. Only an animal would scare his kids."

"Is that so, Dadee?" she asked with nervous movements.

"Yes, that's so, Lena."

"But how do you know, Dadee?"

"Hon, just believe me, parents bring children into this world to love them, not to hurt them." He churned with confidence over his organized conjecture. He sat with her on the couch. "Don't worry, hon. I promise I will always protect you. We have things in common. We both want to end this abuse; we both want to settle accounts with your mother. I'll stay by your side to the end."

Lena's spirit was swimming in happiness.

"How 'bout that!" she rattled.

Before her father had brought up the crime of child abuse she had no idea that it was linked to her disturbing life with her mother. Shifting around in her head now was a realization of that horrid abuse and of its genuine existence. She was remembering her mother shamefully abusing her and she promised herself that she would never give up until her mother's abuse had been completely nullified. She relaxed with her father, intently listening to him, and he was able to briefly lift her spirit to a properly hopeful level, but she was helplessly drifting toward a hated, more degrading stage.

Something much stronger than her drive could subjugate, overcoming the strongest part of her desire. The abuse and putrid environment before her had created in her a strong feeling of unwanted living. A conditioned belief: She was white trash, and nothing would change her stigma of white trash since she was abused and lived in a cesspool!

But, surprisingly, she saw herself above that level of white trash, just because of the impending force of abuse. She was certainly viewed as highly important to her mother, or her mother would not have abused her so brutally.

"Better times are coming, hon," Jim promised happily as he talked over the sound of the television. "Life will soon return to normal, right?"

"I hope so, Dadee," she answered as a mild fear still rippled through all her limbs.

She cuddled snugly beside her father on the couch, knowing that he knew better than she did. She slept to dream. She saw strange men brutally ravaging a helpless mother with glistening buttocks.

She drowsily opened her eyes, uncertain if she was awake, seeing colorful dream figures melting into nothingness, but strangely she had no fear lingering in her.

Chapter Fifteen

A month later Lena watched her mother with emanating happiness and was informed about their summons to court; but, to Lena's disappointment, the news crushed her when Crystal said that she may very well be taken away and put into a foster home, and it was all her father's fault and, in reality, it was he who was abusing Lena and not Crystal. "Now, what do you think of your loving father?" Crystal had asked her weeping daughter. Lena ran to her father for emotional support, questioning him, and demanding the truth and, as she wept, he rationalized the exaggeration of Crystal's statement.

This additional threat triggered more grave fear. The next remark Crystal vented was: "Your father is evil and don't you ever forget that, Angel."

Lena never understood what Crystal had meant and never cared to understand. Of course Lena wanted to believe her, because she wanted to trust her mother, but she knew that was impossible.

Constantly demonstrating signs of ignorance, she saw that her mother strove to disseminate its misery. Her fear of Crystal's ability to harm her invoked her mood into masquerading spasms of deserved respect. The fear of losing her father outweighed the fear of Crystal's abuse. Mommy, I've been at your mercy since birth and you have shamefully hurt me. But if I'm going to be taken away and still hurt, I'd rather you keep hurting me, and I would, at least be with my father too, she thought to herself.

To Lena's imagination a foster home was like a descent into hell, an eternity of fear in which she could be forcefully detained. She wondered how she could ever thwart that hell, and negate that fear. She blinked her eyes in bewilderment.

She felt that the life she was dealing with was not ever going to diminish, and her father's endless encouragement failed to relieve her of fear.

"Lena, there's no sense in worrying because the judge isn't going to take you away from me," he had promised moments before court.

Lena nodded in accord and her limpid hazel eyes were rosy and rheumy.

Before that there had been an intermittent hope of a better life, but now she felt that hope was only a wishful dream. Her mother had seen a weakness in her and decided to exploit it instead of improving it. Why was Crystal always plotting against the family?

"He's right," attorney Scott Armstrong interjected. "Your father has spent a lot of money to keep you with him."

"Listen, Lena," Jim was affectionate. "Get the idea out of your head. You're not going to a foster home." He glanced at Crystal as Crystal bared her rotting teeth at him. He would not admit it but he did feel a tinge of uneasiness. "The judge might put you solely into my custody, so there's no reason to dwell on Mommy's lies, okay?"

"Awright, Dadee. I won't," she said briskly.

"Okay, don't disappoint me," Jim said.

"I won't disappoint you, Dadee."

"All right," Jim smiled, satisfied. "We should be called in pretty soon."

So her father had labeled Crystal a liar while Crystal listened and she had only glared at him. Lena was pensively rolling her father's claim around in her mind. Had he lied there certainly would have been an angry reaction from Crystal. All his words were revealing the deceptive actions of her mother.

The heavy wooden doors to the courtroom opened and a bailiff announced that court was now in session.

"You'll never take my daughter away from me," Crystal hissed, hatefully. "Just wait and see." Her attorney, Anthony Russo, appeared confident and ruthless, and with Crystal's blessings, had earlier drawn up charges against Jim for sexual child abuse. But, of course, the judge laughed it off with Jim and threw the false allegations out of court. Desperate people did desperate things. Russo must have been desperate for money and Crystal desperate for revenge. But Jim overlooked Russo's actions, realizing Russo had fallen into the same trap he fell into with Crystal. He wondered what Russo had done wrong in life to be punished with having Crystal as a client. He probably got what he deserved though. Later Jim had seen him in the Scandinavian Health Spa and gave him the evil eye, and Russo appeared embarrassed and timid and sneaked out the back door. Strangely, they reasoned out their differences and made up, and now worked out beside each other in a quasi friendship. Outside of the courtroom, he even admitted he was shocked at Crystal's behavior toward Lena

Gary Pudaloff, Jim's former professor at Nova University was standing beside Crystal. Jim did not see him physically, but he knew Gary was there because he could smell his bad breath ten feet away. Gary was always friendly to Jim's face but behind Jim's back he was secretly keeping in touch with Crystal. Gary took a disliking to Jim after learning of his nationality. He felt Jim's people were killing too many of his people. But Jim knew something that Gary did not know. The killings were only a tiny sign of what was yet to become of Gary's people. He was the type of person who would shoot you in the back while you were on your knees praying. So Gary was here and he was going to do everything he could to keep Jim from getting sole custody of Lena. He was a great professor but a backstabber for a guardian ad litem. And still he smiled and talked to Jim as if they were still old buddies.

Then Crystal inched forward, her face pale and her movements stiff, with Russo at her side, and twisting his nose at Jim. Lena started after her mother but Jim interfered.

"You better stay with me, Lena," her father advised.

The bailiff's leg, a bloated log, kept the door from closing and her mother went in.

Gary followed the pair like a cat sniffing the ground to see what it could get for free. Jim's eight hundred was not enough and he boasted he was doing the case for free.

Holding her father's hand, Lena sniffed the scary smell of authority; the half-empty courtroom was gripped in a hush and the walls and chairs were frosted with the thick haze of fluorescent lights. She trembled, feeling that evil was lurking in her midst. Smiling at her, holding a briefcase, was Mrs. Rosenblum, blue-eyed and pretty. She and her father took a seat with Scott Armstrong mumbling that he wanted more money from Jim. The judge entered and the bailiff chanted:

"All rise, the Honorable Judge Thomas Lynch presiding."

The judge sat on a big black recliner chair at the head of the long T-shaped table, and his shaggy silver hair and his thick glasses made him look like a simpleton.

"Please be seated," the bailiff said.

The room was now spooky and silent as a morgue. The judge shuffled a thick stack of papers around then glared at everyone to be obedient.

Judge Thomas Lynch listened as his bailiff read off the names of the attending parties

"Lena Smith vs. Crystal Smith and Jim Smith vs. Crystal Smith...Charge: Child Abuse...Charges filed by the State and sanctioned by Mrs. Rosenblum, counselor for Health and Rehabilitative Services..."

"That's us," her father mumbled. "Let's go stand there with Mrs. Rosenblum and your mother."

Lena walked with her father and Scott Armstrong to the T-shaped table where the judge sat looking stressed and incompetent. To add to Lena's plight were well groomed people in suits and ties all staring down at her. Lena now sought security in Scott Armstrong who appeared bored and listless. His thick rippling muscles were hidden behind clean baggy clothes, his blue eyes thirsting for money, easy money from unsuspecting victims. He had once said he felt like he was on a mission to save Jim's daughter's life, but that was just a way to bleed Jim of every cent he had. He cared nothing of the abused child, just how much money he could get out of using his clients, usually by delaying tactics and big talk. Armstrong was so money hungry he had lost his ability to distinguish between reasoning and greed.

Her father was advised by another attorney to dump Scott Armstrong, but that was impossible because Jim had already paid him off. Her father now hated Charlie Leeds, another attorney with whom Jim attended law school, for refusing to help him and for referring him to Scott Armstrong. Jim became suspicious of having the wrong attorney after he had told Jim that a kid being kidnapped, beaten severely, run over, shot in the back by a pellet gun, their teeth busted out, their house burning down, was all part of a child growing up.

"Is this the child?" Judge Lynch asked.

"Yes, Your Honor," Mrs. Rosenblum answered.

Lena felt that an evil hand was about to descend upon her and drag her to the deepest part of hell. She was so filled with dread that she had the urge to clamber underneath the judge's table and hide.

The gray eyed, silver, frizzy-haired judge turned squeamishly to Crystal and Attorney Russo.

"Your husband believes you intentionally and deliberately poured scalding coffee on your daughter's torso. Is that so, Mrs. Smith?" the judge asked.

"Absolutely not, Your honor," Crystal cried into her hands as Russo patted her on the back. "It was only an accident. I poured my niece a cup of coffee...and set it...on the table...and my daughter grabbed it...and it splashed across her chest."

Then Russo took over with earnest effort. He wanted to win the case to make sure Crystal would pay him. "Of course, it was an accident, Your Honor. If you follow the direction of the scald you will see it runs across and down the front of the chest which proves the child accidentally splashed the coffee on herself. The lies, and malicious attack by Mr. Smith appalls us all. Your Honor, you can see for yourself that this child is content, happy and healthy, and is not a victim of abuse at the hands of her loving mother." Then he turned his olive-shaped eyes to Jim in a pretense of grief and his voice sounded full of tears. "How could you do this to your wonderful, loving wife who has devoted herself to you and your daughter? I'm getting sick just thinking about it." Russo felt his pasta dinner churning pleasantly in his stomach. He always believed he was a born actor but just had no opportunity to prove himself. I'm going to win this case and get paid, he gloated.

Jim quickly came alive before the judge could respond. "I know a child abuser when I see one, Mr. Russo. And she's not a wonderful, loving wife. And how would you know she's not a child abuser? The fool thinks everybody is a fool, Mr. Russo. Either you or Crystal is the fool, and I think it's Crystal."

"Listen, Mr. Smith, I told you before that if you couldn't

reason with me, I couldn't deal with you anymore," Mr. Russo stated with a stamp of his foot. "If you have something to say to me have your attorney say it for you."

Mrs. Rosenblum seen Jim was all flustered and came to his aid but Judge Lynch silenced her with a lift of his arm.

Scott Armstrong's words of wisdom were not well received, but the judge listened, but scoffed at his mock effort. He could even tell that Scott was a fraud.

Now Jim gave his speech to which Judge Lynch listened but rolled his eyes back and forth at almost every sentence. "Your Honor, the worse the abuse gets, the more people will not believe it's happening. People only believe abuse when it is presented at a low level because they are too appalled to accept it. Abuse is allowed to run rampant at the expense of the innocent child. It is the legal systems inaction that allows for the abuse to continue unchecked. A child abuser first sees how much he or she can get away with, finding a victim, unleashing an undeserved assault on the child without a reason. All I want to bring to your attention is that if the system allows this child abuser to go unpunished then whatever befalls this innocent child makes you an accomplice to the crime."

Judge Lynch finally lashed out with all the emotion equal to that of a woman, especially a woman displaying incompetence.

"You and your philosophical reasoning is putting me to sleep. Certainly, Mr. Smith, you are not insinuating that I'm an accomplice to an accused child abuser, now are you?" He began scoffing again.

All the time Gary was silent and drinking in the arguments as Judge Lynch waited for his opinion. He glanced at Jim, cleared his throat, then said tersely: "Your Honor, I feel it's in the child's best interest that the mother keep full custody of her."

"Are you being paid for your services?" Judge Lynch

asked premeditatedly.

"As of yet there has been no payment received," Gary said in a tone to get the judge's sympathy. "It's probably going to end up a pro bono case, Your Honor."

"That's sad," Judge Lynch said and he stared at Jim.

Since Jim had given Gary eight hundred earlier, he was confused at Gary's denial of payment and quest for sympathy. Gary was as excellent a liar as he was a professor; he even convinced the judge with his lies. Jim could still smell Gary's rotten breath half way across the courtroom.

Russo had the last word to his delight, "Mrs. Smith is definitely innocent, Your Honor. Right now I can make an unfounded accusation against someone just to attempt to blemish their image but it means nothing if it's not predicated upon any facts. Child abusers are people who have histories of child abuse and we all know she has no history of such horrendous behavior. She's innocent beyond a reasonable doubt.

The judge listened intently, keeping his eyes on Crystal's face. He felt Crystal was not a recidivist.

"That's what I thought. Mrs. Smith, you can keep custody of your daughter, but if anymore such accidents occur I'll relieve you of that custody. I'm leaving the child in the custody of both parents," Judge Lynch stressed. "I'm also offering to send you both to counseling. You both have turned it down before. You can do whatever you want but the offer is there if you decide to accept it." He stood, stuck his tongue out at Jim, and abruptly left the courtroom.

Lena gaped, unable to believe she was going home.

"See? What did I tell you?" her father said as he winked at her.

"I'm just glad it's all over," Scott Armstrong said. That was easy money, Scott thought. I like it like that. But I should have cheated him out of more money.

"He's making a terrible mistake letting your wife keep

Lena," the surprised Mrs. Rosenblum said, draping an arm over Lena's neck and leaving the courtroom with her, Jim and Scott and catching the elevator to the first floor. "The State usually takes the mother's side unless they feel it's a malicious case of child abuse," Mrs. Rosenblum said, apologetically, as Scott Armstrong listened. "Let's hope this keeps Crystal in line."

Scott was silent because he was too busy thinking up ways to cheat more people out of money.

"Sure," Jim nodded, hoping to shield his surprise. "I just can't believe the judge acted so quickly and ignorantly."

Jim realized that not only was Russo and Pudaloff scheming against him, so was Scott Armstrong and Judge Lynch. They all probably got together before court to plot their treachery against him, to make it look like Crystal was innocent and he was just imagining things. They had hung him for nothing and let Crystal go for child abuse.

"Hey," Scott said to Jim, "I can't believe it either. But that's the way the judicial system goes."

He patted the thick wad of hundreds in his pocket he bilked Jim out of.

Jim listened, his eyes drawn and murky.

"He must not have even investigated the case," Jim complained. "How much more malice than second degree burns does the State need to act on the child's behalf?"

"The judge obviously didn't see it the way you and I do," Mrs. Rosenblum explained. "For all I know he may have fallen for her tears, or for any other ungodly reason."

"Yeah, you're right," Jim said, shaking Mrs. Rosenblum's hand.

"Jim, if you're in my neck of the woods, drop by and say hello," Scott encouraged. He could not wait to make more easy money just by filing papers, promising a court date that would never come, giving him endless sympathy but still doing nothing. He was annoyed with Charlie Leeds who told Jim he was a little sleazy and hard up for money. It was the truth but he did not want Jim knowing it because he would not be able to cheat him out of more money.

Absorbed in a vortex of danger, Lena stayed close to her father as they traversed the courtroom lobby. When they got outside the palm trees in front of the courthouse shivered in the balmy breeze. Lena had been impatient to get back outside, so she could feel the humid warmth's skin wrapping her in security. She could sense that from this moment on, the face of life was different; she could feel that that face had resembled her life so closely that she would always distrust its presence. Now she realized that the danger which she had felt was now an intricate part of her. How could she fight it, resist it, or conquer it? Since it was beyond her imagination, she felt even more danger. She could only hope to be relieved of that burden of danger. Her mind was laden with troubles that she refused to allow to subjugate her emotions.

"Lena, you're not in a foster home," her father said.

"I know," Lena said thankfully.

"I think your mother knows better than to ever mistreat you again, Lena," her father said, kissing her forehead. He apparently noticed her nervousness. "You're still scared, aren't you, hon?"

"Yeah," Lena admitted. She affectionately secured her arm around her father's leg.

She looked down the sidewalk and saw her mother.

"Dadee," she looked up at him, "here comes Mommy."

"She's learned her lesson," Jim smiled down at Lena. "I can see it on her face."

"I hope so, Dadee."

The mood to alleviate hostility between her and her mother seized her.

"Dadee, I'm gonna go meet my Mommy," Lena said and

hurried off, recognizing her father's approval by his silence. She broke into a run. Here was the ideal chance.

"Mommy."

Lena plowed into Crystal's legs, hugging them lovingly. Crystal leaned forward joyfully smiling.

"Hi, Angel," her mother said.

"How you doin', Mommy?" Lena's face was flush with happiness.

"Considering the circumstances, I'm doing okay," Crystal answered politely.

"Mommy, do you love me?" Lena had to ask.

"Yes, of course," Crystal laughed.

"I knew it!" Lena exclaimed loudly. Maybe her nightmare life was actually going to improve.

She and her mother held hands.

"You and Dadee won't fight no more, right, Mommy?" Lena asked.

"I would assume not," Crystal said, squeezing Lena's hand and talking so sweetly. "It's better that we get along."

They walked past policemen and attorneys heading for court. Lena waved to her father.

"I feel so good, Mommy," Lena said.

"I'm glad you do," Crystal said.

Crystal's friendliness and the shivering palm trees made her happy to be alive; and it was terrific knowing that she was going back to her dirty shack where the toilets failed to flush down its supply of sewage, where fat rats stalked the floors unchallenged, and where she could play around in colonies of feeding roaches. The horrible odor of shit in the house paled against rat poison sprinkled on the floor like sugar.

"Let's do something nice today," Lena implored with her father, then looked up to her mother.

"Sounds good to me," he told her. "But see if Mommy's interested. I don't want to make her do something against her will."

Her father's talking brought to Lena an image of Crystal touching her, then touching her bad thing and she hated Crystal's telling her to just relax.

"Can we do something nice, Mommy?" Lena asked meekly.

"I guess," her mother said, "we'll stop for ice cream on the way home."

At the State Road 84 exit on I-95 they went west, passing strands of cypress trees, the Secret Woods Nature Center, then, after that, crossed Highway 441 and pulled up to a Carvel ice cream parlor set back from the road. Behind the Carvel stretched a grove of orange trees whose bending branches were heavy with oranges ready for the harvest.

Her head high with the counter, Lena ordered a double dipped chocolate ice cream cone with shining green sprinkles that matched her eyes.

"It sure tastes good," Lena told her parents.

"It looks good," her father said.

"Could get her fat," Crystal said.

"It's okay with me," Lena said.

They smiled. They sat with Lena at a round cement table. Trickles of melted ice cream ran down the cone and across her tiny fingers. She noticed between licks that her parents were avoiding fighting with each other. Lena felt so happy that she wondered if she should be worried about it, but she sensed that there was no reason to be and Crystal appeared happy and that tickled her.

"Don't eat so fast," her father said smilingly.

"She's hungry," her mother said in support of her daughter. She lit up a Kool cigarette and took three long puffs and still no smoke came out of her mouth. Lena wondered where the smoke went.

Lena smiled widely, loving the attention.

"I'm hungry, Mommy!" Lena emphasized in a singsong.

Lena enjoyed it when her mother was in a peaceful mood; Crystal was not herself, but she was better this way. She wondered how long the peace would last. Crystal seemed deep in thought now, and had a look of contained anger. She watched Crystal finally exhale a cloud of blue smoke that lingered in the air.

She finished her ice cream and quickly sat on her hands. Her parents watched, wondering. She leaned her body over to let her chest meet her legs.

"I'm cold!" Lena exclaimed.

"I thought so," Jim laughed.

"You about ready to go?" Crystal asked gently. She did not want Lena to get too happy. She might get spoiled and get out of hand and have to be beaten again.

"Yeah, I guess."

Lena marched happily back to the car. She suddenly threw out her arms in stabbing movements then kicked her feet in a way that imitated a cute dance.

"What are you doing that for?" her mother asked, dropping her cigarette butt to the pavement.

"Because I'm happy!" Lena exclaimed, smiling.

"How nice," Jim said. "I bet you stay happy. No reason not to be."

Chapter Sixteen

Lena lolled on the floor of the dirty living room, swatting big, brave flies, watching mice crawling on the windowsills for food. The sudden sight of the mice gave her an unexpected depression and she stirred uneasily about the rotting shack. She did not mind the spiders and lizards and roaches sharing the house with them. A rabid dog was even at her doorstep one day and she watched as it foamed at the mouth, without thinking anything of it. But for some reason the mice usually depressed her. Her grandmother brought in a big fat alley cat, named Edgar after the famous poet, and it ate so many mice it grew tired of rat meat and refused to eat anymore. Later, Edgar was found dead on the side of the house, and her grandmother told her Edgar had eaten rat poison she had sprinkled down for the rats. It was an accident and it was not her fault. Lena did not show a sign of emotion. She was losing her ability to feel.

Their house was like a zoo; it just was not open to the public or the HRS. The HRS had to force their way in with the police. But no action was ever taken. The HRS were talkers, not doers, just bums waiting for pay checks.

"Angel," her mother's soft voice called.

"Mommy," she smiled. "You just made me feel better. Those big bad rats made me feel bad. I don't like them. They might bite my toes when I go to sleep at night."

"How did I make you feel better?"

"I don't know." She smiled again.

Her gaze fell upon Crystal's grim posture against the filthy walls and she glimpsed the haunted look in her eyes, an evil look that preceded her violent moods she seen in the past, a look that reflected a bad image of herself in a hopeless situation. She flaunted her half nakedness as usual and the crotch of her tight panties creased between the folds of her groin. The happiness she felt collided with her mother's unhappiness, and it kept her full of fear. She was not at all surprised when her mother sat close to her with her legs parted and her face exuding evil; she fondled her daughter for a minute, laughingly, then took her hand and put it to her wet center with soft circular movements.

"You don't mind me doing this, do you?" Crystal asked. Then she fell into a fit of giggling that made her appear benign.

"No," Lena felt compelled to say. There was nothing really funny but she also started to giggle because Crystal was.

"I like to do it," Crystal said between giggles.

"I know." She turned to her mother with confusion. "How come, Mommy'?"

"I'm unsure. Maybe because you're my little Angel."

Lena forced more giggling and looked up into Crystal's eyes. They were demented and yes, her mother was crazy. There was no denying it now. Only this very morning they had been in court and now her mother was abusing her. She knew that this was not an issue Crystal feared, because Crystal seemed bolder now than before. Lena certainly knew that she would always hide it, deny it, because shame still gripped her in force.

"I want to vomit when you do that."

"Just relax," her mother said. She pulled the crotch of

EYES OF A CHILD 153

her panties to one side and Lena's foot touched warm flesh.

"Mommy, that feels nasty." She stiffened fearfully. "I don't like you to do that."

She seemed to ignore her daughter, and she groaned, whimperingly, well, enough to know she was really crazy.

"You'll get used to it," she said.

"Please, Mommy, stop," Lena cried. "I want you to leave me alone."

"Stop whining, Angel," her mother said, making the movements a bit harder and faster. After a few minutes, she stopped but ignored Lena's shedding of tears.

"Thank you, Mommy," Lena said quietly. She saw her past compared to now and reasoned that this second ordeal was much less traumatic.

Crystal was inert, still slightly giggling, the abuse in her eyes overwhelming her nakedness and the stretched marks on her sagging breasts. Lena brought up her knees and wrapped her arms around them.

"You've got the same stuff inside you, Lena," Crystal informed her.

Lena was shocked. She stole a fearful glance at her mother's bad thing and fought down a trembling in her body.

"Mommy, my thing ain't like yours. It's small and dry."

Crystal mocked and laughed and made a few catcalls about her daughter's stupidity.

"That's what you think, Angel. Wait till you get big, you'll see," she mumbled positively.

"I'm big now and I don't have that stuff in me," she said defensively.

"Time tells all," Crystal said mockingly.

Lena knew Crystal would always do this to her and she wanted to get away from the abuse, since her hate for Crystal was on the rise. It was so painful when Crystal had mentioned that they were alike. Wiggling her foot until the anxiety declined, the piercing pains of shame and humiliation dominated her. The thought of flight entered her mind; could she convince her father to take her and vanish? How had her mother become a child abuser?

"Mommy, did your Mommy ever touch you?" she questioned directly, boldly.

"What?" Her eyes turned sad and she turned to Lena with paleness on her face. "No, my father did." She twisted a little and righted her panties.

"Why."

"He must've liked me." She paused. "Yes, my Daddy loved his baby with those glistening green beads for eyes. That's what he told me. He never lied in his whole life."

"What did he do to you?"

She paused again, blinked her eyes as more sadness poured into them.

"Everything," she said bluntly.

"Did your Mommy know about it?"

"You really don't wanna know?" She became agitated.

"Yes I do, Mommy," she said as a sadness also crept into her green eyes. "I just want to learn all about you."

"Sure, my mother knew all about it." She fell into another fit of giggling.

"What did she do?" she asked.

"She told me not to tell anybody," she confessed. "She kept it a secret and made me do the same."

"How often did your father touch you?"

Crystal hesitated, her eyes now as sad as eyes could get.

"How often didn't he touch me is what you should have asked. Very often," she said matter-of-factly.

"Were you scared?"

"Terrified."

"Do you hate him?"

"Of course not. How can you hate your father'?"

"Did you tell him to leave you alone?"

"Never. No reason too. My mother didn't care so neither did I."

"Poor Mommy," she said almost crying.

A wind whispered against the windowpanes. Crystal appeared like a ghost in the gloomy shack and her elusive nature could not have been more apparent.

"It's nice to have you with me," Crystal said, slumping next to her daughter.

"I would have told your father to leave you alone."

"Why?"

"So you wouldn't be scared."

She stroked Lena's hair, her eyes brightening.

"I lied, Angel," she admitted. "I was never scared. My Daddy would never hurt me."

That upset Lena. Her mother justified her father's actions. She cared less of the abuse, overlooked the torment she had suffered while at his mercy. Lena realized Crystal had learned to live with that abuse, had accepted it, but she would never accept it. And she was confident. She had to learn to live with it, because it was part of her life; but she would not accept it, because that would mean she had also justified it. She felt that only a fool would justify the actions of an abusive person and whatever fool did justify abuse would be a bigger fool than the fool who was the abuser and she could never let that happen.

"Where's your father now?"

Crystal rubbed at her vagina and giggled again.

"In a cemetery."

Lena giggled too, then suddenly looked confused.

"Mommy, what's your father doing there?"

"He's resting," she spoke profusely. "Yeah...That's where we buried him. He died in seventy-three."

"Ohhh, he's dead." Lena spoke uneasily.

"Yeah, he died in seventy-three," Crystal said in a nostalgic tone that hinted at relief, "and I killed him."

"You did, Mommy?" Lena asked cryptically.

"I sure did," Crystal said, her giggling turning to tears now. "I killed him sure as hell. My mother had to work at the Salty Dog Bar and told me to give him his medication at nine. I forgot. I was eight years old and just forgot." Crystal wiped tears from her eyes. "At ten I remembered and went to his room and found him gripping his chest. He was dead, and I killed him. It was all my fault."

"It wasn't your fault, Mommy," Lena tried to speak like an adult. "He probably smoked himself to death like you're going to do."

That seemed to slacken Crystal's grief. "I would rather have my father abusing me and alive, than not abusing me and dead."

It was probably Crystal's guilt that made her accept her father's ways. She seemed unable to distinguish if Crystal was happy or sad that her father was dead. Lena felt that Crystal's abusive moods robbed her of her decency of motherhood. She sighed deeply at the thought of Crystal's father's death. Lena realized her mother had simply ignored the abuse, but she found it impossible to ignore. She was prying into Crystal's childhood because she was compelled to find a link between Crystal's abuse and herself, her life. Her mother had abused her because she was a dependent child unable to protect herself. A mother birthed an innocent child and, since it was obvious that the child was dependent, the mother could freely abuse that child. That child, years later, would birth a child and would instinctively abuse her child. So, Crystal was abused and now she abused her child. Lena's abuse was starting to make sense.

"I wish you would have told your father to leave you alone," Lena told her.

"Angel, it didn't matter," she said sadly, quietly. "Nothing mattered anymore. My own flesh 'n blood mother didn't care. So I didn't care."

Lena just lay back, thinking if she would have to wait till her mother died to be left alone? Probably so. Her mother, helpless like her, had been an innocent victim living in an abusive world.

"You wanna hear in detail what he did to me, Angel?" Crystal asked.

"No," she cried mentally.

Crystal moved and stood in front of the screen door; and, in the gloom, she appeared frighteningly abusive. Lena now felt that she was being abused because of Crystal's father.

"You seem in deep thought, Angel?" she told Lena.

"I know," she said.

The outline of her naked mother against the transparent screen gave the appearance of hopelessness.

"Mommy, did you ever like it'?"

"Did I ever like it'?" she repeated crudely. "Sure. What made you ask that'?"

"I was just wondering."

"Do you like it?"

"I don't think so."

"You probably do," Crystal said seriously. "Matter of fact, I know you do. Crying and all that stuff is only telling me you like it."

"It is?" Lena's eyes bulged widely. If only she had known.

"Of course it is. It's so evident. Sooner or later you'll admit it."

She abhorred the way she intentionally put words into her mouth. She was baffled at how Crystal was so natural a child abuser.

"No I won't," she retorted, shaking with anxious anger.

"I bet you will."

"You want me to admit to a lie?"

"No. Only to the truth. That's all."

"I'm so glad you want me to tell the truth."

Crystal's eyes flashed slyly.

"I know it's hard admitting things about yourself." Crystal stood sadistically before her daughter. "You know what I mean?"

"I don't think I ever will."

"Why not?"

"Because you're confusing me," Lena said regretfully. She bowed her head sadly as tears stained her cheeks. "That's not fair."

"There's no place for those tears," Crystal said. "Why are you always crying?"

"You act like you don't know," she said with a sob. Even though she had been sad that Crystal had been abused, it meant nothing to Crystal. One moment she was sad for Crystal, then the next moment Crystal had her crying.

"I don't think I do," Crystal told her.

Lena sat up and restrained her crying.

"What were all those questions about my father for?" Crystal asked. "He's been dead and buried for over twenty years."

"I'm confused, Mommy," she said to evade the question.

They were giving each other the evil eye. The sound of the rats scratching inside the walls sounded like fingertips running across the keys of a rusty piano.

"Mommy?"

"Yeah?"

"Those big bad rats give me the chills."

She pulled up tightly on her panties then sat beside Lena.

"Hold me, Mommy," she said.

As Crystal pulled Lena on her lap, Lena turned to her and bit angrily, vengefully into her neck. She was not a vampire but she could bite like one. If she were going to be abused, then possibly, by fighting it herself, she might hinder its intensity. She still loved her mother, but still feared her.

Chapter Seventeen

After the less frightening ordeal with Crystal, Lena found herself idling listlessly in her bedroom, ignoring her toys, and gradually succumbing to the abuse of Crystal, who, delightedly, showed no remorse for taking advantage of her helpless daughter. Lena had to control her emotions, to offer pity when Crystal complained, to masquerade a silly concern for her miserable mother and, when Crystal approached her, she would blurt singingly: "Mommy, I know that if your father didn't hurt you, you wouldn't hurt me...." Then she would lie back unresistingly while her mother abused her. "Whatever you want to do to me just do it, and I won't complain, because if I do I know you'll bust up my teeth for a third time," Lena often sang. That abuse made her feel a weird type of importance. She had become Crystal's victim and she still sought to escape it. Crystal encouraged her daily to justify the abuse, to blot it out of her mind, to accept it as just a fact of life, to confide in no one but her, and to lie to everyone, especially to her father. Thus Crystal made it Lena's goal to ensure that the truth was never disclosed.

All through the year Lena, yielding to Crystal, was abused constantly. She knew that by not complaining to her father she would just continue to suffer. In her bedroom, while watching flies and gnats swarm about a sack of reeking garbage, she sensed soft footsteps and she naturally shifted her gaze. Her father filled the doorway and Lena smiled. Sensing an interrogation, she appeared indifferent, seemingly amazed at the gnats swirling in a tiny funnel. He wrinkled his brow and glanced about. Lena's face flushed. How could she attest to more misery? Well, her continual abuse was probably no secret. She was thankful that it had not been worse.

Jim loomed over her with questions on his mind

"You've been hanging around in your room for a long time now," he said.

Lena looked up. He was blinking in dismay at the garbage.

"Oh, not too long," Lena countered.

"Why have you been isolating yourself, Lena?" he questioned her bluntly.

"Because I like to," she said.

"I want you to start playing out in the living room," her father said.

"Awright, Dadee," she wanted to please him. "But, why?"

He stared at her. Lena could tell that more questioning was coming. She looked at the gnats again. "Mommy seems to be pleased with you," he said.

"Yeah, I know," she said, acting ignorant. She hoped that her indifference would cover any idea of abuse.

Jim, appearing thoughtfully above her, blinked disbelievingly.

"Sooner or later I'll definitely find out what's wrong," he said.

"Nothing's wrong, Dadee."

"When Mommy's nice, something's wrong," he said flatly.

"Not so," Lena defended.

Would he force her to talk? Would he take her back to Mrs. Rosenblum?

"You seem like you don't care about anything, hon," he

told her.

"So?" she said, twisting her hands.

"Your disinterest makes me think you don't even care about yourself. I can see a change in behavior

"I'm okay," she said, still twisting her hands.

She sat on the dirty floor for another minute, then, to please him, she went obediently to the living room. Glancing over her shoulder, she saw her father right behind her.

"Just keep walking till you're on the porch," he said. "We can finish our conversation out there."

"Awright," Lena moaned, only half indifferent now.

She felt that her father knew that her mother had still been abusing her. She stood on the porch, wondering what was coming next. She felt nervous and she quickly decided to calm his suspicion of abuse by continuing to deny that anything was wrong. She still did not know why she lied about it. Her father stood by her with a grieved look. Then, he kneeled down to look her in the eyes.

"Your continuous listlessness and seclusion tells me that something's wrong, dead wrong."

Seeing how suspicious he was, she just stared at him. Timidly, she shrugged her shoulders.

"Nothing's wrong that I know of, Dadee."

"What do I have to do to make you realize I'm here to help you?" her father groaned.

"You tell me that all the time, Dadee," she kept evading.

"Don't you realize that I know that something's not right with you?" he asked sadly, shaking his head pleadingly.

"Things are right with me."

"I would bet you that they aren't."

"I got it," Lena finally cracked under her father's interrogation. "You think Mommy's been bothering me."

"Right," he said.

She knew that he knew about the abuse, but he failed to

know exactly what type of abuse it was.

"Does your mother beat you, starve you, or does she tie you up and put you in the closet and listen to you scream?" Jim questioned with anger. "I can tell just by watching you that she's doing something very rude to you."

"Not so, Dadee."

"Like hell," Jim argued. "I'm on to something that is real! I've been wanting you to tell me about things, but you won't! You're not acting right, Lena. Jim blinked his eyes quickly. "Are you stupid? Crystal will kill you and make it look like an accident."

Truth turned Lena's legs weak.

"Why, Dadee?"

"I don't know why she'd kill you, but I know damn well she would."

"You know a lot, Dadee, and I'll tell you whatever is true," she lied skillfully. She was about to cry, but did not know if it was from Jim yelling at her, or from the lie to him that she would speak the truth, or from a fear of death.

"How has Crystal abused you?"

"She always talks nice to me, Dadee. My Mommy would never hurt me."

"You're just not old enough to tell on your mother yet. You'll talk after she breaks your legs."

"Yeah, huh, Dadee. Mommy would never break my legs. She's concerned about me and—"

"She's abusive, and you have to realize it," Jim complained. "No one knows it, but me! I hate an abuser of children. I'm trying to save your life!"Jim suddenly smiled and pet Lena's head. "I wanted you to live to at least adolescence."

That jolted her, because she hated the thought of death.

"I don't ever wanna die," she spoke clearly. Then said plainly: "I'm small, Dadee."

"That's it," Jim said and blinked. He stood on the grassless yard and studied the impassive look on her face. He yelled. "Maybe you think that all this is just a joke."

"No I don't, Dadee," Lena pleaded.

"You still want me to help you?"

"Yeah," she responded quickly. Her response had been so insincere that she felt guilty. Then she became sincere. "I don't want you and Mommy fighting anymore." She pleaded with her eyes.

"If you keep denying everything, I'll think you're playing games with me and I won't help you no more!"

"I'm not playing games with you, Dadee," she said. "I've made mistakes and I know it, Dadee." She stopped talking and gathered herself. "I'm scared that's all."

"Lena, please stop selling yourself short," Jim pleaded. "I want to help you, but you have to let me. If you don't let me you're just tightening the noose around your neck. I was hoping you could see the light. Lena, aren't you concerned about yourself?"

"Yes, Dadee."

"Then why lie to me?" Jim asked bluntly. "It makes no sense to lie. Lena, you've really disappointed me." He looked real sad.

He looked about to cry and that hurt her as deeply as her mother had hurt her.

"I'll never disappoint you again, Dadee. Okay?" she said, trying to placate him.

"I hope that you don't," Jim said with so much anguish that it surprised Lena.

"I'll stop lying." Lena promised. "Lying is bad!"

"I already confronted Mommy," Jim told her. "She swore she was not mistreating you. She accused me of trying to start trouble. Lena, I can offer help all day, but if you don't accept it it's useless. I can't see how you can tolerate being an abused child but it's in your hands."

"Dadee, I don't want to be 'bused," she stressed. "I just had to be reminded."

"Okay, then we'll see, hon," Jim said, jingling his key chain. "Your lying only hurts me on the surface; but it hurts you deep down, but you don't know it." He smiled and patted her head kindly. "I gotta get a nap. Think about things."

"Awright, Dadee. I'll tell the truth."

Her father went inside. She idled on the steps and thought. Definitely, she would talk. Movement rustled behind her. She looked around. Her mother joined her.

"Lena," Crystal said.

"What," Lena answered meanly.

"Angel, I don't really care," Crystal explained. "But he's trying to make you lie about me."

"I don't want to hear no more, Mommy," she yelled.

"Don't say that I didn't warn you about him and his deceptive approach."

"I won't," Lena glared.

"Your Daddy is evil."

"Sure," Lena mumbled. She was full of hate that she wanted to unload on her mother. "He's not evil, I love him."

Crystal's eyes widened.

"I see it's impossible to get through to you," she said and started back inside. "You're stubborn and stupid like your father."

She was disgusted with her mother. She thought about her parents' moods and nothing seemed to make sense. Why were her parents always bickering? Could it be that her mother needed a blind person to lead so she could confirm her own blindness and her father did not fit the description? She blinked, realizing at last that she would accept her life as it was. She glanced at the store across the street and she longed for a cherry Popsicle. She thought, then decided. She could taste that savoring cherry flavor on her tongue.

"I'm going for a walk, Mommy," she called into the house.

"You're a big girl. Do whatever you want."

She listened, filling with anxiety, seeing how much her mother cared.

I don't care either, Lena thought and started off.

Chapter Nineteen

They headed home with Lena summoning ways to spite Crystal. Lena wished Crystal had noticed her absence, had learned a lesson, and had missed her, but she already knew that when she got home Crystal would, at once, play down the issue that she had run away.

They opened the door and caught Crystal as usual chain smoking, gulping black coffee, wallowing in the filth of the house and watching a horror movie. Between the filth and the horror movie, Lena did not know which was worse. And Lena never understood what inspired Crystal to indulge so deeply in smoking. But happily, Lena realized, that Jim was about to open a conversation based upon her running away.

"I bet you don't know that your daughter ran away, Crystal," Jim mumbled, stroking Lena's shoulder length brown hair.

"She's always running off somewhere," Crystal complained, unmoved by Lena's brief disappearance. She continued to gloat at a screaming vampire about to sink its fangs into a victim's jugular vein.

Lena pictured her mother as a skunk that just sprayed a foul odor. Crystal apparently felt that Jim was insinuating that she was a horrible mother by neglecting Lena.

"Some nut could have stolen her from us." Jim felt that

if Crystal ignored him further, she was passing a death sentence on her daughter and she was the executioner.

"But that could happen right here inside our house," Crystal protested.

Lena stepped between her parents.

"Dadee, we just got home, and I'm tired. You and Mommy be nice now. We should be happy for a change. I think we can if we try. I know it's not so easy to be nice."

"Listen to her, Jim," Crystal belched.

Jim's eyes almost popped out of their sockets. Lena was six years old and she had made more sense than both him and Crystal.

"I'm going to get a drink," Lena said. "When I get back I don't want to see no fighting now, please?"

"That's the way I always wanted it," Crystal said.

"Okay," Jim nodded, shocked that Lena had made a tentative peace in the house.

"Relax, Dadee," Lena said, playfully motioning him to obey.

"Good girl, Angel. You're just wonderful," Crystal complimented.

Lena saw her mother puffing on her cigarette like a fiend. When she had smoked it to the filter she quickly lit up another one.

"When you and Dadee wanna fight, just let me know so I can break it up," Lena urged her mother.

"You're nicer than us," her mother said.

When Lena brought her attention to her father, he folded his hands together politely.

"I'm impressed. You're the best mediator in the world. I can't make peace no matter how hard I try and you made it look simple," Jim said, pleased.

"You gotta try, Dadee," Lena said candidly. "You and Mommy just never try."

Chapter Eighteen

Meekly, Lena's sixth Easter arrived with her responding critically to the impossibility of ending her abuse. She had never really expected it to completely end, but as it gradually intensified she became aware that she was confronted with a perpetual problem. As terrible as it made her feel she finally admitted that she hated her mother. She did not see herself as organically hateful; she had long tolerated her mother's abuse; she was just dismally aware that what her mother did to her deviated from the normal trend of living.

She suddenly succumbed to the scariest thought of her entire life. She was preparing to run away and leave behind the pangs of abuse. She felt, timidly, that her decision was less scary than what her mother did to her. She could only remember of being kept indoors, like in a prison cell where the legal system had never ventured.

After eating her lunch, she quietly filled up her thermos jug with raspberry Kool-Aid and wrapped a cherry jam sandwich. She was sweating when she reached the neighborhood park, and, to her shock, her father was pensively sitting on a swing.

"Lena, you want me to push you on the swings?" Jim asked.

Lena was sullen, ashamed; his following her to the park

made her feel that he could read her thoughts before she acted.

"No. Not now."

"Hon, I have to tell you about something wonderful," Jim told her.

"But I'm not running away forever," Lena said.

"It has nothing to do with running away," Jim said gently.

Lena felt sad; her life stunk to that of other kids. At that prison called home, she would be abused, and she did not want to tolerate it anymore. She whined when her father took her thermos and led her to a bench under shade trees.

"That's right, I'm not talking about running away," Jim said again. "Because, it's not that important right now." He faced Lena with a wide smile. "Hon, next summer I'm going to Michigan to study law at Thomas Cooley law school and I'm taking you with me."

Lena felt a jolt, a spark of hope.

"Where's Michigan and Thomas Cooley law school?"

"Way up north near the North Pole," her father said, smiling wider.

"You mean where Santa Claus and his reindeer lives, and where it snows candy canes all the time, and where people freeze like icicles?" She thought of a sky filled with falling candy canes, and Santa's reindeer licking her mint-scented fingers.

"That's what I mean," Jim laughed.

"I don't think I understand," she said, thinking fleetingly of a wonderful life at the North Pole.

"Hon, listen to what I'm saying," Jim said. "I'm going to law school."

"But why? And when did this happen?" Lena asked.

"I got my letter of acceptance just now," Jim said.

"And you're taking me with you, Dadee?" Lena squealed. "You taking Mommy too?"

EYES OF A CHILD 169

"Nope. She's no good," Jim said flatly.

Lena's sadness surprisingly escalated. Sure, she hated her mother and she wanted to escape the abuse, but somewhere in the deepest corridor of her heart she was repelled by the thought of dumping her. Wow, and law school might have nullified the abuse, but she still indirectly felt love for Crystal, and so Lena opted to stay with her mother. She started softly whimpering, regretful of the distressing urge to inform her father how vague instinct made her choose to stay with her mother. Jim quickly disrupted her deep thoughts.

"I figured you'd be happy. But I didn't expect you to cry," Jim laughed. "Hon, we're going to have a great time."

"Yeah. I bet. Oh, no, Dadee," Lena whined.

"Don't be silly," Jim taunted her. "The door to a better life has opened."

"I don't want a better life," Lena moaned. "I want my Mommy."

"Once you're away from your mother you will love it," Jim said.

"I don't want that," Lena told him. "I thought I did but I guess I didn't."

Her father stared anxiously in her eyes.

"If I leave you behind you'll sooner or later run away from home again," Jim said.

"I'm still not going," Lena pressed. Her refusal had devastated her father's goodwill and she opposed him with her stern hazel eyes. "And I'm not sure why," she said and she shook her head slowly and sadly.

"Staying with Crystal could be fatal," Jim warned.

"It's better than never seeing my Mommy again," Lena said.

There was nothing she could do. If she stayed with her mother she might die. If she left with her father she might not ever see her mother again. Lena did not know which was best. She believed she wanted to be free of her mother, but strange feelings made her think otherwise. She had faltered in her own eyes, her father was leaving for law school, and she was rejecting the opportunity to leave behind her abusive mother. She was more confused than ever. She no longer cared about herself.

"That makes sense, since you only have one mother," Jim told her. "Even if she is a child abuser."

"You're so understanding, Dadee," Lena sang happily.

Okay, she had fought against help, stiffly opposed her father's golden offer. Her mind was clotted with confusion as she told him. "I'll write!"

"Crystal's done poisoned your innocent mind. She's molded you into believing that bad is good and good is bad," Jim said sadly.

"But I'll definitely straighten her out," Lena said; she was wishing a wish that only came true in dreams. Her mother was beyond repair.

"She's ruined you, my daughter, for life," Jim groaned.

Lena was ultimately ecstatic, she would return to the slum shack to rot with her rotten mother.

"I'll miss you so much," she told him.

"Right, Lena."

"I really will," she promised her father, standing anxiously in the park. She hid from her father the fear of losing him. "I want to go home now, Dadee!"

"Yeah," Jim smiled, nodding his head. He gave her a big hug and pet her on the head: "Hon, you've got more brains in your little head than me and your mother put together."

Fate had accelerated her drive to show her father that she would be safe with her mother, would easily survive, would control Crystal's abuse, and, since she was six, she practically understood her life. After Crystal got reabsorbed in her movie, Lena spoke bluntly.

"I need to talk to you, Dadee."

"I hope it's something I want to hear," Jim laughed.

She confronted him with her shoulders pulled back. "I want to go with you, but I'm scared, real scared."

Jim noticed his daughter's posture. He decided not to oppose her, nodded, then his eyes watered.

"Yes, I know," he spoke in a yielding tone.

"I just can't help it, Dadee," Lena explained. "I don't want to leave my Mommy yet."

Jim stared. Lena realized he was now full of understanding.

"I can't leave you, Lena."

"You mean you still don't trust Mommy with me, Dadee?"

Jim felt his throat lump like a brick and said:

"That's right, Lena. I don't fully trust Crystal with you."

Anxiety forced Lena to stir uneasily.

"I know, Dadee!"

"Just relax, Lena, it's a while before summer's here."

"Oh, good."

"Look. I have to give you another lecture."

She waited, with confusion making her feel dizzy.

"I wanted you to live a better life. But if you want this it's your decision. How can you be happy while always under the threat of abuse? And I don't need to say anymore. You can stay, okay? But you'll regret it. And if you don't remember what I'm saying, I'll scream you to death."

"Awright, Dadee."

"I'm putting it to you straight because I care about you."

"Dadee, I'll always listen to you," she said.

"Ignore Crystal. She's treacherous. She will do her best to hurt you by neglecting you till you put yourself in danger. Don't believe anything she says. Don't trust her. Don't provoke her. And be careful."

"Awright." She promised with all her heart.

"Good." Jim smiled, then kissed her. "Someday, I'll get you away from here, but if you want to stay, then stay."

"Awright, Dadee."

Bloated with pride, she swam in it. Her words had been respected. Her father was certainly understanding. He had warned her of deception, betrayal, hostility with her mother. She was learning everything to be learned from a learned teacher. I'm the most fortunate kid in the world, she thought, exalted. I'll be on guard against Mommy. I'll handle her by her own games. She could now plot against her mother at will, especially if it was to her detriment. At least I now stand a chance, she thought again.

Chapter Twenty

And it all came to pass. From that time on, without any signs of mercy from Crystal, Lena was neglected until she was in danger, before Crystal gave her the needed attention; then her anxiety was so bad she could not appreciate it.

"You gotta tend to yourself," her mother laughed at her. "You should be vegetating in your room. You're too immature to come out. You're stupid too."

The weekend abuse was even more appalling. She had to supervise and feed herself, yielding to Crystal's warped mentality, disgusted at the sight of filth on Crystal's body, raw sewage overflowing from the toilets, and Crystal's lice ridden hair; noticing Crystal showering once a week, always prancing about in skimpy panties she seldom changed, usually scared and beaten; wishing to ignore the repetitious arguments over her father, poverty, morals, and her lifeless sex life that fell on the rocks.

She would constantly ponder how to manipulate her mother, subduing her abuse and controlling her; then, at other times when peace seemed possible, Lena would rush excitedly to her mother's room, seeing her sleeping naked.

"Get up, Mommy," Lena would whisper, gently touching her shoulder. "I love you."

After a gradual body movement and a few groans and

moans, her mother would scream miserably:

"I don't give a damn if you love me. What are you doing waking me up this early?"

"Just wanted you to know I was awake," she would whisper cautiously.

"You can never do for yourself," Crystal would complain angrily.

"I just want you to be nice to me, Mommy," Lena would plead timidly.

"I am nice to you, you little bitch," Crystal would groan. "I see you're a little loony like your father. How did I ever get mixed up with that educated old goat?"

Lena would pretend futility not to be scared.

"I'm playing out front in the dirt where Dadee parks the car," Lena would say as a way to get away from her mother.

"I could care less where you play," Crystal would bitch. "Matter of fact, I hope you get run over."

"Some day I'll run away and never come back," Lena would threaten.

Then more bitching would start as her mother angrily climbed out of bed and, wavering sleepily on her feet, stark naked, clutching a pair of soiled panties to slip into, her beady green eyes flashing anger and her shapely Anglo white, fleshly body standing above helpless Lena.

"That suits me just fine," Crystal would admit. "Now get, you ugly bitch, before I get a knife and cut your heart out. I'm not about to watch you now, nope, not today. You should be watching me for being your mother in this filthy, rotten wooden shack your darling father provided. I'm better off sleeping out in the street. And I'm not feeding you today or tomorrow. You're getting fat you lazy rat.

"Have it any way you want, Mommy," Lena would whine, turning and leaving the house.

Proud Crystal would blend with her filthy room where

the ceiling would be peeling; the walls would be stacked high with junk, and garbage; the curtains rotted on its frame; every inch of the squalid room packed with decaying items.

Lena would play, squeamishly thinking, hearing that stupid talk, feeling quite sad, appearing dumb too, and constantly dreaming that some day she would be bold enough to leave.

"I wonder why Lena loves to roll in the dirt?" Crystal would talk aloud, but acting like Lena did not hear her. "Maybe she's a pig! Yeah. That's gotta be it!"

And Lena would listen tensely as her mother kept up the badgering.

Her mother would creep out on the porch and she would stand perfectly still, then turn to Lena with hateful ridicule.

"Why are you playing in the dirt? Who told you to play there?" she would ask.

"You did," Lena would finally cry, lowering her face into her tiny hands.

"Angel, I'm only playing," she would lie when she felt a slight pity for Lena, and then deride her again.

Lena would watch, blinking her eyes, regarding her mother strangely through her tears.

"Angel, you are definitely stupid. I just think you're confused," Crystal would say.

Day in, day out, Lena would experience her mother's unwavering strange moods, and it alarmed her.

Why would her mother treat her bad all the time? But she deliberately hid the idea that she felt Crystal's abuse crazy, for her father had alerted her that revealing the truth could bring on more abuse.

"Lena, I've no concrete idea why your mother treats you bad," Jim had said. "For her, it's normal, just a way of life. That's all I can really say."

A week later, annoyed and dismayed, Lena finally approached her father.

"Dadee, staying with Mommy is absolutely terrifying. My Mommy is crazy, Dadee. She's gotta be because all she ever does is act crazy. And she never stops."

"Lena, ignore her behavior. Pay no attention to it. Your days of staying with her are numbered. When you finally get fed up with her, you'll suggest that we leave. So stop paying attention to it. She's a sack of stupidity."

Lena winced at her father's reasoning as she thought about what he had said. What she absorbed from Crystal made her think that her mommy was living in another world. She noticed in Crystal a bristling listlessness, a deliberate stupidity, a simpleton's mentality with a limited intellectual capacity concentrating on hate and abuse, on misery and self-pity. She did not understand Crystal's urge to abuse her without any genuine cause or reason. Her abusive life still flourished with assaults against her innocence: mental cruelty, injury, molestation, neglect. And I've withstood it all, she complimented herself.

Still not fully understanding, she started to realize the horrible life Crystal led was unnecessary; tragically, things went sour for Crystal, but she could not pinpoint it, and Crystal wanted to take it out on her. An abusive mother with a troubled imagination had delightedly brought misery upon her and made her feel inferior about herself and her life, and she could not determine the reason why that mother had ruined her life for her. While painfully absorbing her mother's abuse, Lena still had, deep inside, a compassion for Crystal. Though she lived with her mother, tolerated the abuse, she could still feel in her a throbbing sense of superiority.

Lena became stoic to the abuse by a crazy mother, displayed a strange silence to the pain she suffered, was silently outraged that she bad been robbed of her self-esteem and pride, and tried to control driving feelings of flight. She usually related to her father as new events occurred. And, as those terrible incidents became vivid memories, Jim approached her, saying:

"Lena, hon, you're growing up faster than any normal child. It's sad yet it's good. I underestimated your level of tolerance. I let you make your decision about staying with Crystal and you knew what you were doing. I'm impressed with your ability to think for yourself. I guess you know what's best for you. I'm so happy. You made that transition into independent thinking, something most poor people can never do," he said.

"Thank you, Dadee," she said happily. Her transition in life had been incidentally achieved.

Chapter Twenty-one

She suddenly wondered of her future with her mother. She wondered if she should change her mind and leave with her father. Or keep tolerating the abuse and attempt to work with her mother? She felt dazed with indecision. As she thought, her mother quietly encountered her.

"Something is going on behind my back," Crystal complained.

"Really?" Lena acted surprised.

She smiled meekly and headed for her toys. Her mother, exhibiting her naked breasts, stalked her like a predator preparing for a kill, her green eyes searching Lena's face.

Lena readied her mind for Crystal's attack; she felt dreamy when she saw the crevice of Crystal's bad thing. "I don't know what to tell you, Mommy," she said.

"You should." Crystal stared ominously and scratched her crotch.

"I don't know what you mean." She sat on her choo choo train and a creak told her she had outgrown it.

"Angel, you do know what I mean," Crystal said.

"Awright. If you say so, Mommy."

Fearing what she knew Crystal had alluded to, could provoke more abuse, she now prepared herself to resist her mother to the best she could.

"You and Jim's plotting to leave me, right?" Crystal asked.

"Not that I know of." Lena denied knowing of Jim's actions and sounded unconcerned. "Mommy, leave me out of your problems. Please, Mommy? If Daddy's planning to leave you then that's his business. I don't know anything."

The green of Crystal's eyes deepened and hate reflected on them.

"I think you know more than you act, Angel."

"Yeah. I bet you do."

She had to find a way to escape Crystal's cruelty. Crystal was a witch, but Lena meant bitch, but did not want to think it because profanity was bad; that was what her father told her and she promised him she would never say it.

"I still can't believe you," Crystal said. "Jim confides in you and don't try'n deny it. He'll tell you everything and won't tell me anything. See, Angel, if you know something that I don't know, you better speak, and I mean now! I need this trouble like I need a hole in the head."

"It sounds like you already got a hole in the head, Mommy," Lena countered.

Crystal looked like she was about to pounce on her defenseless daughter.

"Yeah, I know you're Jim's daughter," Crystal mumbled. "I couldn't deny it if I tried. You're a wise ass just like him."

Lena knew she had to manipulate her mother to prevent herself from getting a beating.

"I know nothing, Mommy!" Her legs trembled and her teeth chattered. "Leave me alone. Stop pickin' on me." Held-in anger and dread forced her to claw at her mother's leg.

"You do that again and I'll break your arm," Crystal promised. "You're a big girl now and I want you to act like one."

The hate in her mother was unbearable and her teeth kept chattering. Even though she was staying, she was staying at her own choosing, and she contained as much hate against her mother as her mother had against her.

"Angel, did Jim tell you that he was going to take you away from me?"

"No, Mommy."

"Did he say he was leaving?"

"No, Mommy."

"Did he say he wanted to take you to a better life?"

"No, Mommy." Lena wrinkled her brow in alarming surprise. She tried to go for a roll on her choo choo train but the wheel broke.

"Stop playing with me, bitch. You're learning to deceive me just like Jim."

"You got things wrong, Mommy!"

"What secrets has he been sharing with you?"

"None."

"I can see lies all over your face."

"Mommy, why bother me if Daddy's leaving you. Why don't you just ask him?" Lena questioned her.

"Yeah." Crystal was brooding, angry, afraid she might lose her meal ticket. "That's just what I'll do."

"Good," Lena was satisfied.

"Did Jim say anything about going back to school?"

"Huh, uh, Mommy."

"I see I can't trust you either."

"Mommy," Lena wished Crystal would leave her alone, "I don't know nothing." She lifted her hand to claw at Crystal again then stopped.

"Go ahead," Crystal said. "I'll rip that arm off your body."

How was she ever going to get her mother off her back. She could only imagine how funny she would look to other kids after having her arm ripped off.

"Mommy, how many times do I have to say I don't know anything?"

"I bet you do."

"It's too bad you feel that way."

"I wanna know what's going on," Crystal argued in a crazy mood.

"I don't know anything."

"Angel," Crystal was fuming, "if he leaves me, well...I'll leave you."

Lena could hardly believe what she had just heard, but she could tell her mother was serious. She now sensed the possibility that she might leave with her father after all.

"Then I'm sorry for myself, Mommy," Lena almost cried. Even her mother wanted to leave her. She felt all alone.

"You think I would do it?"

"Considering the way you've been acting lately, yes."

"So you think I would do it?"

"Yes," she said and her little hands shook.

"Angel, listen to me: I'm laying down the law. Jim's not going anywhere. He's staying here with me, below rock bottom. But, God forbid if he sneaks off on me because I'll damn well sneak off on you. You'll wake up one morning and never see me again. So if you know anything you had better speak up." She then sneered sarcastically: "Education. A better life. What nonsense. So, Angel, I hope you have something to tell me."

"I don't," she was steadfast, her anxious face glowing. Despite her fear, she was enjoying jerking her mother around.

"Slow down and think."

"There's nothing for me to think about, Mommy!" she protested with a scream. Her chattering teeth had almost clamped down on her tongue.

"I said to slow down, Angel," Crystal said. "Lena?"

"What now, Mommy?"

"I can tell when you're lying," Crystal swore.

Her chattering teeth sounded loud to her. Her mother was

easily seeing the truth hiding in her mental depths.

"I don't lie and you're saying I'm lying, Mommy," she deliberately lied to spite her mother even though that was the only time she lied.

"You're a liar," Crystal insisted. "Because I'm a liar and you're my daughter. And you've been with Jim too long."

"That don't mean nothing!" she defended. "I know you're a liar but that doesn't make me a liar."

"What do you mean? You claim you're not a liar like me, but I know you've been lying through your rotten teeth, right?"

"Wrong!" She yelled at Crystal and Crystal took her by her hair.

"Come on now, talk, so I don't have to break all your bones," Crystal laughed at her daughter.

Lena felt her hair coming out by the roots, resisting silently. She was afraid to claw at Crystal, because of Crystal's threat to rip off her arm. Getting a beating or getting her hair pulled out was bad, but losing an arm would be horrible. She closed her eyes and prayed. Then her hair came out by the roots and her mother gloatingly bit into her ear until it bled. Lena blinked, rubbed her scalp, felt her bleeding ear, but remained totally silent. Her tears and feelings were becoming a thing of the past.

"I think you're enjoying the pain," Crystal smiled. "I'm going to decide to kill you later."

She let Lena's hair fall to the floor, laughed, and touched Lena's bloody ear.

"I've told you the truth, Mommy," Lena argued back, hating her mother more.

"No, you haven't!"

"Uh, huh, Mommy."

"What's Jim plotting?"

"Nothing! Nothing," she mumbled, remembering him tell

her that he was leaving for school.

Crystal listened crazily. Lena felt that Crystal might beat her, a beating that could make her pulled out hair and bleeding ear look like nothing. She would defeat her mother and all her stupidity combined.

"Mommy?" Her voice was heavy with grief.

"What?"

"You hurt me."

"Oh well. Too bad." Crystal paused. "No, Lena, you hurt yourself."

Lena rubbed her scalp, touched her ear and saw blood on her fingers, and saw the reality of life melt before her eyes.

"Right here on my ear is where you hurt me most, Mommy."

Crystal pulled back her straggly hair. Deep hate separated them. Lena now avoided looking into her eyes, because she feared Crystal might kill her. Crystal had lost all rationality and most of her human values.

"Why you sneaky little bitch," Crystal mumbled. "You're trying to get one over me, but I won't let you!" Crystal looked at the bloodstain on her fingers, then said softly. "I better wash my hands before I get hepatitis. I bet you're wishing I'll get it. Even if I'm dying I'll never let you or your father get the best of me." Crystal's irrationality mounted.

"I'm really sorry I ever birthed you. I never wanted you. I should've aborted you. Life was great until you came along." Crystal grabbed a heavy detergent and began washing her hands.

Lena, disturbed, resumed her attention on her choo choo train and saw before her a bleak future.

Chapter Twenty-two

She stared pitifully into the humid night, crying. A realistic thought hung in her mind; staying with her mother would mean certain death. She better leave with her father now. But the thought of dumping her abusive mother still made her sad. It seemed that the worse her mother became the more she hated to dump her. She had developed hostile ties with her mother from the abuse but she still had not developed enough control over her hatred that would make her turn on her mother.

Could she force herself to leave with her father. Yes, but, she would never ever see her mother again, and she believed she needed her. Oh, if only she could leave she would eventually have a better life. But the uncertainty of a new and different life scared her.

Sure, she could dump her mother, but she was also worried of what might become of her. Without any means of support her mother could end up sleeping on the street. Or her mother could end up being ravaged by a strange pumping man. Definitely, she had to stay with her mother to see that nothing bad happened to her.

Gloomy daylight filtered into her bedroom. She had a throbbing headache and the skin on her limbs ached every time she moved them. She gently stretched her legs; it soothed them momentarily. Familiar movement in the house made her happy.

"Dadee," she said happily.

Her father stopped and stared, smiling but dragging, kissed her. She hugged him.

"Lena, how nice of you to meet me at the door," he said.

"I've been waiting here for you all night, Dadee," she said, smiling.

"If that is true, hon, then something's wrong."

"It's nothing new, Dadee," Lena countered quickly.

Lena wrapped her arm around Jim's leg. Lena felt safe now. Great, he wants to know what's wrong.

"Lena," he spoke quietly, "just tell me what's wrong and I'll decide if it's out of the ordinary."

"Mommy's been questioning me about you," Lena explained in a cautious whisper.

Jim cursed angrily but quietly.

"It doesn't surprise me," Jim said. "What did she want to know?"

"If you were going to leave her," Lena whispered. Fear claimed her.

"I can't believe it, hon. That just disgusts me. I don't know how much more of this I can take."

Lena put a tiny finger to her lips. Her father had constantly informed her about her mother and yet she never listened. She knew she would regret it and, since it was obvious the abuse would get worse, she wondered about her decision. Depression overwhelmed her fear now.

"Mommy questioned me over and over again," she told him.

"Hon, just stay out of her way," Jim encouraged.

"I try to," she complained. "It doesn't work though. I don't know what to do."

"Try and keep at a distance from Crystal," Jim advised.

"She could hurt you. I'm concerned about your safety!"

"But Mommy comes after me all the time," she explained.

"Then come with me," Jim coaxed. "Crystal will never change her evil ways."

"I'll change her evil ways, Dadee," she defended herself.

"I hope so," Jim said seriously.

Lena's anxiety got the best of her and she pulled at her hair with her fingers.

"Relax, Lena," Jim said passively. "There's not much for me to say, because you chose to stay with Crystal. But I'm proud of you for handling her so well."

Lena had listened suspiciously, wondering if her father was really proud of her.

"Hon, there's still time to come with me," Jim assured her.

She listened pensively, wondering if she would ever again see her mother.

"If we leave, how long will it be before I see my Mommy again?" she asked him.

Jim kissed her head as she waited for an answer.

"Only a year," Jim urged her.

"No. That's too long!" Lena groaned.

"Six months." Jim was bribing her.

"No." Lena was still determined to stay.

"At the end of the first semester." Jim was desperate to free her of her mother.

"No. I'll stay with Mommy. I might cry if I leave her."

She had the shelter of her mother and her father was urging her to leave that shelter. If she left, she would not be able to smell raw sewage anymore, nor would she hear rats scratching inside the walls anymore, nor would she see her mother walking around naked and dirty and bitching all the time. In a sense, it was quite depressing.

"I'll bring you back at midterm," Jim promised, his desperation peaking.

"I'm not going with you," she said bluntly.

"You'll regret it," Jim said.

"Forget it, Dadee," Lena pressured him. "Please?"

"Okay, hon," Jim agreed. "You know what you're doing." He smiled, his movements slow and tired from working all night. "You be careful." He pet her head. "I'm going to sleep, Lena."

"Awright, Dadee," Lena said.

Lena stood in place as Jim blended into the gloom; her mind was drained of all hope and she pulled harder at her hair in a mood of fear and helplessness. Should I leave with him? she questioned herself. After her father left she would be totally trapped. She would be at her mother's disposal. She was an abused child in a hopeless household. It was not so bad, she tried to convince herself. She felt sick at her stomach. She could not leave her Mommy. She was part of her Mommy. Then she wanted to sleep this nightmarish indecision away. Maybe she would be here forever.

The realization that she would probably stay made her feel smug with security.

Chapter Twenty-three

Months lapsed. And before Lena knew it another Easter arrived and she was still rotting in the shack, accompanied by her despairing father. At times she would strip off her clothes and walk naked outside and stare at passing cars honking their horns.

"You don't make sense to me no more," Jim complained. "You're not acting right. Something's wrong if you go outside with no clothes on. Maybe Crystal's turning you crazy too. It's possible, you know."

As Crystal had seen Lena naked many times, she made no effort to remedy the problem, and actually encouraged her to continue it.

"Lena, Crystal loves to see you dirty, naked and nasty," Jim told her. "She can easily relate to that style of life, Lena, because she identifies herself with it. So stop pleasing her."

"Dadee, I'm never going to go naked outside again," Lena would promise sincerely.

"If you give in to bad habits, you're endangering your chances for a decent future," Jim said.

"How could Mommy hurt me?" Lena questioned sadly.

"She thinks it's a good way to get attention. But she's really trying to hurt me. You know it's bad, so don't act like her. You know she's crazy."

Jim struggled on a daily basis to mend Lena's moral structure, but whenever victory was almost within reach, Crystal would hatefully undermine his activity.

"I'm sick of her," Lena crackled. "I'll hate her till I die."

"I can relate to that, Lena," Jim listened to her. "That makes plenty of sense. Your mother will never change."

Her life had been so bad that she seemed to be smothering in a cloud of confusion. Not a day passed without feeling a deep concern for her safety. She would find a way to pay back the anguish she suffered at the hands of her mother. It was just a matter of time. Crystal gave Lena a short reprieve from the abuse. Her father informed her that he was taking her mother back to court. The thought of living in a foster home only added stress to her troubled mind. Lena was confident now that when her father was leaving that she would change her mind and leave too. She dwelled upon the thought of leaving. It would devastate her abusive mother not to have a victim. Still she did not want to make her Mommy sad and would probably not leave.

Despite the plight of her abusive life she had always hoped to change it. She was baffled how her father tolerated her mother while she, who also tolerated her mother, found it unbearable? Had he tolerated her mother for her sake? She knew that her father's concern for her would prevent him from disclosing the truth. Could he have understood her mother's peculiar behavior well enough that he tolerated her, held compassion for her? Her father's inherent awareness, an awareness sharpened by life's experiences, had put her mother temporarily in place. The thought of wearing his shoes after he left was unappealing to her. She had been victimized without any apparent reason but regardless she was overly willing to stay with her abuser.

Her father's departure was secretly planned for spring but, when the time came, he never left. He explained to Lena's relief that it was unjust and unwise to leave her behind at Crystal's mercy.

The warm weather brought her back outdoors. She played bleakly, realizing her mind was empty of happiness. What had really motivated her mother to abuse her? She thought through her anxiety, vividly remembering that incident when Crystal had beaten her unconscious and she awoke to find Crystal touching her. In her wildest dreams she never would have believed that could happen to her and strangely she now wanted to relive that incident to never forget that moment of horror Crystal put her through. She should have resisted when her mother had come to her, and it could have slackened the severity of the abuse. But, stupidly she had resigned herself, obedient, scared, crying, unwilling to accept that her own flesh and blood mother, the person she trusted the most, would do this to her.

Crystal's abuse was so inhuman that Lena was constantly in fear of it. In the animal kingdom offspring were treated like her, but in the human kingdom it was not supposed to be that way. And as much as she hated it, it kept getting more out of control. She could not understand why her mother treated her the way she did. Her dilemma became more complex, more puzzling, more emotionally devastating than anybody could imagine. She was helpless which made her feel more vulnerable. Crystal had forced upon her rules that she had to follow; rules that would label her as white trash, as a liar, a justifier of abuse, a condonor of abuse. And Crystal's flagrant abuse seemed to poison her perspective on what the world was supposed to be, on what the world was supposed to represent, not a place of abuse where a sick mother could exercise power over her child. Lena could not understand the abuse, had never wanted to. A fleeting sadness swept through her as she realized the concern for her that had made her father give up his law school opportunity.

Maybe she would beat Lena to death and get nationwide publicity like Baby Lollipop's lesbian mother got. The lesbian also got the death penalty but she never burned. Crystal could get Lena an outfit with lollipops on it, but she was probably too old for that. Maybe she could get Lena an outfit with bunny rabbits on it and toss Lena's stiff body on the roadside like Baby Lollipop's mother did to him, and she would become known as Baby Bunny Rabbit, and she would deny beating Lena to death and beat the charges. She considered herself much smarter than Baby Lollipop's mother. Much smarter than the Zile's and Smith's and scores of other child abusers.

"You're scaring me," Lena whined. What's wrong with you?"

Crystal crouched as though she were about to violently leap on Lena with the coat hanger. Lena looked for an escape route. The front door was locked and she was starting to panic.

"You and Jim were mistakes in my life," Crystal groaned. "And I aim to correct those mistakes. God, the hardship you brought upon me!"

"Maybe it's my fault that I was born," Lena told her. "You know that, Mommy?"

"Yeah. No, it's my own damn fault," Crystal admitted. "You ain't as funny as you think, Lena."

"You're acting violent today. Don't hurt me," Lena begged.

"Tell me why I shouldn't," Crystal said, inching toward Lena. "Tell me."

"Awright. Just give me a minute," Lena stalled.

"I don't like waiting," Crystal complained, approaching Lena as she slowly backed away. "Hurry up. "

"Because it's not right to beat on me without a reason."

"I need a reason to beat on you?" Crystal asked her.

"That's right," Lena sought boldness.

"Since when did I need a reason? I make the rules in this house," Crystal spoke nastily. "You're mine. "I'll do whatever I want with you and nobody can stop me."

"But it'll be nice though right, Mommy?" Lena asked, her concern rising.

"Not sure yet. I'm never sure. But who cares."

Lena backed away from Crystal in fear. Oh, oh! Crystal was implying to her that she was going to beat her with the coat hanger.

"Someday I'll be sure of myself though," Crystal was full of sadistic brutality.

Lena was about to run to unlock the door but Crystal leaped and snatched her by the hair before she could move and the force of Crystal's grip slapped her down like a pancake, banging her face on the floor.

"You little cunt bitch," Crystal shrieked, gripping the coat hanger and beating on Lena's head before she could run. "I'm gonna kill you this time!"

"Don't, Mommy," Lena screamed.

Crazy, ignoring Lena's plea, Crystal slammed the coat hanger all over Lena's tiny head, back and arms.

"Yeah, I'm gonna kill you," Crystal laughed.

Lena begged again and again, swinging her arms to try and hold back Crystal's deadly beating. A shower of glass shattering on the floor told Lena that her father had crashed through the front door.

"That's enough, Crystal," Jim yelled.

Lena gasped in horror as Crystal raised the coat hanger toward the ceiling and brought it down with such force that the wire cut into her scalp as she screamed and covered up, praying, hoping her father would intervene. Then Lena could wait no longer for Jim to save her and made a crawling dash underneath an end table, determined to reach shelter alive. But Crystal grabbed her leg and pulled her back out as Jim finally jumped on her.

"Stop beating her, Crystal," Jim shouted.

For not responding he slammed Crystal against the wall. Lena cowered beneath the table, choking, groaning, too scared to come out on her own. Crystal slammed the coat hanger against Lena's tiny feet as a final goodwill gesture.

"I should kill you both!"

"Touch her again, and I'll kill you," Jim promised. "You're proud of yourself now, aren't you, Crystal?"

Lena looked up with bloodied head at Jim opposing Crystal with clinched fist.

"Please help me, Dadee," Lena pleaded.

A hateful groan came from Jim's throat.

"You're plotting to kill my daughter, Crystal," Jim accused.

"That's right," Crystal admitted. "I'll kill you too."

"Stay out of my sight," Jim said, slapping Crystal hard on the head. Then he grabbed her around the neck and choked her till she jolted and screamed. He seen a butcher knife on the table and seriously considered cutting Crystal's throat, but held back because Lena had suffered enough.

Jim struggled to get Lena out from under the end table, then held her in his arms. He lay her down on the couch, her head bruised, her face bleeding in veiny trickles. Her mind was filling with hate, shocked that her mother had attacked her so cruelly. Lena's fear quickly diminished as she, aching and whimpering, was helped by her father.

"Crystal's really crazy," he told Lena.

"She sure is," Lena still whimpered.

"Why did she do that to you?" Jim asked.

"If you don't know how would I know?" Lena said.

Jim cried, hugging his daughter.

Lena mourned for herself for demonstrating stupidity. As usual she wanted to rationalize with her mother, understand her, coax the coat hanger from her. But now she was starting to show that same stupidity that her mother showed. Quite obviously her mother's behavior was rubbing off on her. She had had ample time to flee before her mother beat her, but had waited until it was too late. Why would she not wake up? And would her mother be a child abuser for ever and ever? Santa Claus was not going to bring her no toys this year.

Lena suddenly stiffened then jumped into her father's lap. Jim was startled. Then Crystal was beside them.

"I'm sorry, Lena, for being bad to you," Crystal said.

"Awright, Mommy," Lena said, staring dazedly about. She sounded like she forgave Crystal but was only acting like she did because she felt she had to. She wondered when her mother would beat her like this again. She brutalizes me because she knows she can get away with it, Lena thought.

"You oughta be," Jim lashed out. "I should report you to the police."

"Go ahead," Crystal mumbled. "It doesn't matter?."

"The best thing I could do for you is to kill you," Jim said.

Crystal stared silently at Jim.

Lena was so insecure that she would not leave her Father's side. Her head ached unbearably. Her hair was a mat of drying blood. Jim inspected carefully her lacerations and a little later decided to take Lena to the hospital. Coincidentally, Dr. Ehrlich was the emergency room physician. His cold blue eyes studied Jim thoughtfully and suspiciously. Dr. Ehrlich explained that the X-rays showed that she suffered a thin skull fracture. A twenty-four hour hospital stay was advised by Dr. Ehrlich and Lena was assigned to a room in the pediatric ward.

Jim had lied that Lena had fallen down a stairway to avoid having the incident reported to the police. He was certain that no action would be taken against Crystal, anyway. Matter of fact, she would blame it on him and the authorities would possibly believe her. Unknowingly to Jim, had it not been that Dr. Ehrlich liked him he would have alerted HRS authorities for possible child abuse. But he knew Jim would not hurt anybody, much less a child. Only cowards hurt children. But from that day on, Dr. Ehrlich was not as friendly and his visits to Seven Eleven declined drastically. When Jim asked why, his only excuse was that he stopped smoking and did not want free coffee anymore. Even when Lisa showed up, Dr. Ehrlich only smiled at her and quickly left and he had always been very fond of Lisa.

Midnight descended, but she wanted to stay awake. She relaxed, recuperating in peace, victimized by a life of abuse. Feeling better, she blinked her eyes and thought. She was lost, in the hands of a mother who had no soul. Crystal had inherited an innate skill to make her a victim and get away with it. Crystal kept brutalizing her and she kept suffering because she would not fully confide in her father. She lay, sweating; a feeling of helplessness suffused her and she whimpered.

"I'd leave now if I could!"

Chapter Twenty-five

Only a couple days passed before Lena was back out in her front yard playing in the dirt. She tried to ignore her mother who was standing on the porch watching her. Lena wondered if she had any remorse as she stood there.

"It's such a peaceful day, Mommy," Lena said.

"It sure is, Angel," Crystal said. "You Mommy's friend?"

"Yeah," she lied with deep conviction.

Crystal luxuriated in the warm sunlight, and surprisingly started smiling.

"Are you happy about something, Mommy?" Lena asked her.

"Yes, very much so," Crystal said kindly. "You've grown up and now you don't need me anymore. I'm free at last."

"Mommy, does that mean I can do anything I want?" Lena asked. "Like go across the street all by myself to get a Popsicle? Play in the road like the other kids, throw rocks at passing police cars, and actually come and go as I please? Maybe even get caught up in a drive by shooting and play with dope along with the white trash?"

"That's right, Angel," Crystal confirmed.

"Will Dadee approve of it?"

"Angel, I'll handle him," Crystal promised.

"Awright," Lena agreed. "But he might not go for it. He's

worried that I could get hurt by being on my own. He said you gave him enough grief as it is."

"Listen, Angel," Crystal concluded, "I told you I'd handle him."

"Awright, Mommy."

Lena watched her go back into the house. She knew that Crystal had never cared about her. She had always been without her except when Crystal abused her.

She would dump Crystal if ever given another opportunity and she would be treacherous like Crystal and keep silent, in case Crystal would try to prevent her leaving. She now regretted her abusive life more than ever; she now felt more helpless than ever; and she now hoped for a better life more than ever.

Lena gazed through the screen door at Crystal, and a fiery hate flared in her mind. She had been cheated, defeated, abandoned. It was wrong. She had been brutalized too long. Part of her childhood was lost. She felt her face become a mask of burning anger.

Crystal had not even come close to being a decent mother to her. She would wait for the time to turn on her to punish her. She played in the dirt with a deep, lingering loneliness. Crystal had always abused her. But she had to ignore it. That was the past. Crystal's being her mother would not make her forgive her. Crystal's abusive disposition toward her, a disposition that had blinded her to reality, would someday come back to haunt her. If she ever had another chance to leave she would do so without a trace of regret. Let her mother rot all alone. She hoped Crystal would burn in hell with the other child abusers.

Chapter Twenty-six

Shortly after another Easter came and went, on the eve of Lena's seventh birthday, her father interrupted her Frazzle Rock show. That was unlike him. Something was wrong. She had been absorbed in the puppets, at their jerky limbs, at their squeaky voices, then finally she looked at him, drenched in worry, her head feeling so light that she was dizzy. She could feel the bad news, hoping that it was not as serious as she felt.

"Sorry for bothering you, hon," Jim apologized to her soothingly.

"That's awright, Dadee," Lena said.

"I see you love your Frazzle Rock, Lena," Jim smiled.

"Yeah, I sure do," she said.

"That's nice," Jim returned in a pacifying tone.

"I know," Lena said firmly.

"That makes me happy for you," Jim said.

Lena's worry that her father had bad news was slowly vanishing. Introductory conversation in her living had always intimated about what was yet to come; the climax of the issue came through a series of events. She relaxed, sensing that things were not critical as she had imagined. Jim stood over her, petting her head.

"Sorry for interrupting your favorite show, Lena,' Jim apologized in a sincere manner.

"Oh, that's okay," Lena confessed with a wondering look.

"You're so sweet," Jim said. He kissed her on both her cheeks. "Hon, that was terrible what your mother did to you with that coat hanger."

"Yeah, I know, it really hurt," Lena whispered. "I cried because she hurt my feelings more than my head."

She wished he would hurry and tell her what he was driving at. Her light-headedness persisted.

"Lena, hon," Jim said. "You're a real honey. You've stood your ground with Crystal every inch of the way."

"Yeah," she mumbled. "I probably did." She heard her favorite puppet talking now.

Jim smiled and cuddled closer to Lena

"I'm not scolding you, Lena," Jim said, "but you chose to stay with Crystal and look what happened?"

She realized that he meant that each time she was abused the abuse merely got worse. She wished he would not have reminded her.

"I made a bad decision, Dadee," she admitted

"But you realize it," Jim said. "That's the important thing!"

"I'll never make the same mistake twice," Lena vowed. She had crossed her heart.

"I don't think you will," Jim said knowingly.

Lena felt pleased that he still had confidence in her.

"Has Crystal been bothering you?" Jim asked.

"Not lately."

"Has she been neglecting you?"

"Always I guess," Lena said.

"Did she say that she may be back in court?" Jim asked.

Lena's face exhibited much concern. She still sensed the reality of being detained in a foster home.

"No," she said. "She's not said a word."

"She's a dirty animal," Jim stressed. "You're too good for her."

"You're right, Dadee," she agreed in haste.

Jim kissed her and, with his muscled right arm, picked up Lena. She gave him a hug, knowing instinctively that there would be no bad news.

"Lena, I'll never let no one ever hurt you again," Jim said with tight face.

"Thank you," Lena answered.

Jim put her down and stepped back. Lena's suspicion rose. Had she misjudged? Her legs weakened. Was there something wrong after all? She waited meekly for him to speak.

"I want to be away from your mother now, Lena," Jim said, quietly. "I'm sorry for it. But I hate nightmares."

Lena's legs strengthened now. She stared into his eyes, expecting him to encourage her along.

"So you're going to leave, Dadee?" Lena said in a innocent voice. She studied him with suppressed fear. "But I'm not staying here without you."

"I know you're not," Jim said. He stroked her brown curls affectionately. "I would never leave you behind. We'll leave together tomorrow."

"Awright."

"Aren't you happy?"

"Of course, Dadee."

"Then why are you looking at me blankly for? Maybe you didn't understand."

"Tomorrow we'll leave?" Lena squealed.

"That's right. I'm getting you out of this pigsty first thing tomorrow," Jim said.

"Awright."

Lena stood still, silent, pensive, not believing that it was really true. She was unable to react happily, for lingering guilt still tormented her, but she did not want to disappoint her father either, because that could signal that his efforts were not appreciated. The impact of her leaving finally descended fully upon her. She blinked her hazel eyes then tears of happiness fell across her cheeks.

"Your gratitude is recognized," Jim said. "I had to let the abuse go this far so you would know where you stood with your mother. I didn't want to take you away too soon because, later in life, you might think I was trying to deprive you of your mother, and that would never happen."

"Thanks," she said and really meant it. And that was all she wanted to say.

Jim knelt to her and she hugged him again.

"I'm getting you out of here whether you like it or not," Jim said, smiling.

It was like she was emerging from a pool of glue that had trapped her for so long as he confirmed her leaving. Despite her tears, her grief, her eyes emitted true satisfaction.

"Okay, Lena. Get back to your show. I won't disturb you again," Jim promised.

"It doesn't matter," she mumbled.

"Of course it matters. Finish watching Frazzle Rock."

"No. I'm too busy thinking of the good days that's ahead of me."

"Now that's a smart girl," Jim said, still smiling.

She blinked at the sensation that her congested mind had strangely cleared. Her life was already shedding its pessimism and budding afresh with an optimism that she had never experienced, had never known existed in all her life. She felt now that her mother had missed all the precious things in life: compassion, happiness, harmony.

"You still haven't told me why you're looking at me blankly for. Maybe you don't want to leave."

"I'm just happy, Dadee," Lena gasped.

Relieved, Lena stood there, seemingly oblivious of Jim and her show.

"Is something wrong, Lena?"

"No. What time are we leaving?"

"Late in the morning. You know I sleep late."

"Awright."

"Now get back to your show, hon."

"Awright."

"You're the sweetest thing in my life. How could such a cruel animal for a mother birth such a precious child? I'll never know."

"And neither will I, Dadee."

As Jim walked away, her innocent appearance took on a look of supreme happiness. She turned her attention back to the television, thinking uncaringly of abandoning Crystal. Finally it was all over. She was happier than her bunny rabbit, happier than all the bunny rabbits in the whole world, even as the image of Crystal's bad thing made her shiver. Damn Crystal. Good riddance to her. Let God condemn her sick, amoral mother to hell. She was more than ready to leave in the morning. She would no longer acknowledge Crystal's existence. She would dump Crystal, happily. If Crystal questioned her, she would lie, lie, lie. Her life now was drifting back toward reality as it had been before the incident with her mother in her bedroom when abuse had turned her life into a living hell. She would not wish that horrible nightmare on her worst enemy.

Lena folded her arms together, pondering the disgraceful secrets in her mind, secrets that she assumed she would never reveal even to her father. She was still so ashamed of them that she still could not tell him everything.

Lena still pondered. Could she ever really live a happy life? Was there a life after an abusive life? And if there was, could she be happy with all the horror hidden in her heart. Most kids had come to life and had lived in happiness. She had come to life and had lived a nightmare. As her mind kept getting clearer, life kept on gradually displaying more reality. It was dawning on her that her life was more than a nightmare. How had she ever survived it? She just knew she was no longer going to have to live it. And, logically, she was telling herself to leave behind the nudging pain of her abusive life.

Chapter Twenty-seven

At dawn next morning Lena crept into her mother's bedroom for a last glimpse. Crystal was sleeping heavily while she gazed at her. Hurt filled her heart. She yearned to be with Crystal but yearned to be free of abuse. Unable to control her emotions, she wept freely, silently. Almost without realizing it she wet her panties, the urine trickling down her leg and puddling on the floor. The painful likelihood of leaving her mother forever was unbearable so she turned and her little legs led her away, ever so slowly.

A moment later, she found herself in the filthy kitchen, wiping her face dry of tears. She looked vaguely about at piles of fetid garbage where overfed, tan colored rats feasted heartily, then sat on her knees beside them and meticulously rummaged through it until she came upon a lump of dead roaches, decaying on moldy wet bread. She stared at the roaches for a long time then without fully understanding herself, and as a rat squirmed in protest, she took a little of it's food at a time into her hand and rubbed it on her face, arms and tummy until it was all on her. Then she caked it on her lips but did not eat any, because it was dirty.

She did not know why she did this, but just felt like doing it by an overpowering desire.

She did realize though that her action was somehow related to her life.

She stood, feeling the slime on her skin drying. She just stood there, still, only her eyes moving, staring strangely at the pale light reflecting gloomily off the rats and the garbage strewn across the kitchen floor. She felt as if she had been in the kitchen for years. She did not understand herself and she did not try to. Lena, at length, went to her bedroom. She climbed back into bed and lay back on her pillows. Waves of sorrow crashed on the shores of her mind. She struggled vainly to dispel the intruding force of her consciousness. Lena pulled her blanket over her face and cuddled up to it tightly. Never had she experienced such tormenting discomfort. She must have dozed off without knowing it. When she opened her eyes, a golden sun, more beautiful than she had ever seen before, was lighting her bedroom.

She was very sleepy and could have easily fallen back to sleep, but the savory thought of leaving prodded her to her feet. She pulled on her dirty pants and went in search of her father. She found him in bed sound asleep. Deciding not to awaken him, she felt it enticing to go outside to play in the golden haze of sunlight.

She unsnapped the door lock and her bare feet stepped out onto misty ground. How lucky she was to be leaving behind the dreadful abuse. She was amazed at how the sun had drenched the streets and walks in lustrous gold. She was fleeing a life that she had hated and that had psychologically traumatized her. Had she stayed, could she have ever made her mother realize how she had destroyed her life with hate and abuse? Probably not. The type of life she had lived and would always live was only proper to her mother. Should she not just accept her abuse and tolerate the life that her mother had given her? Should she not just believe, as her father believed that her mother was abusing her to get at him, and pretend that her abuse had never occurred? All in all, she was ashamed of the life her mother had given her. Moreover, she did not have the power to protect herself against the abuse, for her spirit had been brutally broken. She saw before her the dawning of a happy life and was drawn relentlessly toward it. The ability to lie came not from a desire for deception, but of survival. Realizing that she was finally fleeing the torment and abuse, she could now see far enough into life to assume that her life had been a replica of her mother's life.

She climbed up on the hood of the old car and her eyes settled on the huge trees in the front yard that stood before her like thick skeletons. Her mother sat in the living room chain smoking. A light cool breeze caressed her face. The feeling of true peace was in her. Birds chirped. Flowers sprouted. All the vegetation in the yard was an unusually beautiful green. The sun's color deepened. She saw her life at this moment as wonderful. The fairyland look of her surroundings held her in mute wonder. Warm sprinkles on her flesh made her look about and she saw gold dripping from the trees and shack. The sun was raining gold. She felt silence descend and engulf her world in true peace. All overtones of evil had left her.

The smudge of a gold car sloshed silently through puddles of gold. Liquid gold even dripped from the roof of the store across the street. The thought of a Popsicle came to her. A gold Popsicle. She dropped from the car to the ground without hearing a sound. She saw a woodpecker soundlessly hammering away on a tree trunk. How wonderful this world of gold silence was. How had she ever wanted to leave? She looked back at the store then for her father. Yeah, she would hurry across the street and get a Popsicle before he got out of bed.

In her haste, she failed to look both ways, lowered her head, then dashed for the store. The loud roar of an engine suddenly broke her world of silence and out of the corner of

EYES OF A CHILD 211

her eye she saw a gold car almost on her. She knew there was no chance to avoid being hit. In vain she ran harder. Her gold world turned black as the speeding car slammed into her tiny body. A pitiful scream charged with horror escaped from her lungs.

The car held its speed, rounded State Road 84 with a loud squeal, and disappeared.

She was thrown as high as the treetops. A desperate plea for life came to her as she sailed over telephone wires.

Could she grab on to the live wires and live? She came down violently on the top of her head with an awful crunch. It sounded like a sledgehammer banging against concrete.

A passerby near the store looked at her broken body then walked off with a Budweiser in his hand. A big beat-up Buick full of neighborhood trash drove around her, angry that she was blocking the street. Finally a Good Samaritan stopped his car in the middle of the road so that she would not be struck again by passing cars.

DJ came upon Lena, his face a spot of white horror. He recognized her smashed head and made for her house in a rabbit-like sprint. He began banging his fists frantically upon the screen door.

Crystal came to the door with a lit Kool cigarette hanging from her lips and saw that DJ's eyes were tinted with fright.

"Lena's deader 'n a rock," DJ gasped. "She got hit by a car.

Crystal calmly took a deep puff on her Kool. Jim, half asleep, heard DJ and his body stiffened. At first, Jim thought he was having a nightmare with his eyes open; then he thought he was hearing dream voices. Then he was fully awake and a vivid image of Lena's tiny body splattered in the road pounded in his brain. Shock instantly launched him into a catatonic state but he shook it off; then he bolted out of bed and started running and screaming for his daughter, brushing past Crystal and DJ. Trembling, he paused in the dirt yard, to make sure he had not just lost his mind. He started flaying his fists in the air as he saw people huddling in the middle of the road. He ran to them still screaming, knocking them away. God...there she was. She was flat on her back with her big green eyes toward him,--she condemned him for not acting quickly enough to save her life--her head caved in so that the top was flat. Blood still spilled from her busted head. The nerves of her left leg made her kick like she was trying to get up. He fell into a world where he only saw himself and Lena. Lena was gone. She had gone out in a smear. Crystal had won.

He knelt beside his daughter, crying, cuddled her up on his lap and kissed at her bloodied and broken head. He suddenly heard footsteps and, with bloodstained lips, he saw Crystal beside him, his heart crying out for his daughter's life. He squeezed Lena affectionately to his chest as though he had already accepted that it would be the last time he would ever do so. He turned his head to the bank clock that was a block away and was shocked to see that it was 10:36 A.M., then turned back to Crystal.

"You realize...it's her birthday today. She'd be seven...at this very second...if she'd lived," he cried to Crystal.

Silently, Crystal scratched a flame from her lighter and lit another Kool. All that seemed to matter to her was a good smoke and a good way to get his goat, and she found a good way by sacrificing his daughter. The stupid girl had spent her whole marriage trying to get even with him for something he knew nothing about. It was so stupid he never even bothered to ask her about it. Deep down he could not condemn her fully because he knew he was very instrumental in creating this animal called Crystal. He had given her a child, the only important thing that ever happened in her life and she thought

EYES OF A CHILD 213

it cute to exploit it.

Terrible tremors swept through his body as he again realized that Lena was gone forever. Softly, he lay her body back on the road and stood up, facing Crystal. She blew Kool smoke into his face. She had to prove her dominance. He raised his hands to his head in agony. Impulse dictated his actions now. The relentless wailing of sirens could be heard far in the distance. His hands fell back to his sides. He kept staring at Crystal then back at Lena. The intense pain in him was palpable.

When he had a baby with her, it was like signing a contract with the devil.

"You wanted her dead!" Jim accused Crystal. He glanced sickly at Lena's body. "Why couldn't that be you!" His breathing was laborious. His eyes dimmed as if the blood of life had stopped coursing through his veins, as if there had been a lack of energy to make it flow. "Why didn't God take your life instead of my daughter's? You're the one who deserved to die, not her. All she ever wanted in life was to be happy and play with her toys like any other child."

Crystal again remained silent. Jim saw that her mind was empty of grief, concern, her eyes fixed in a way that had long invited disaster.

"You killed my daughter. Lena's own flesh 'n blood killed her." He knelt over Lena again and wept. "Your mother killed you, Lena! I pray to God that you understand that even in death!" He stood back up to Crystal, screaming. "Do you realize that you killed your daughter! Sure you do, but you don't care! I know you wanted her dead !" He looked into the bright sky momentarily, then screamed to God to send down death and claim his soul too. "You've killed me, Crystal! You killed me through Lena! That was what you wanted all along! Lena's death was just a pawn for you to get even with me for a crime I never committed!" He lifted his arms and eyes back to the sky, his face covered with sweat. "You plotted Lena's death before she was born! I saw the evil in your eyes when you were pregnant! You came to her as a curse! Why did she ever get cursed to have you as a mother! You're nothing but a filthy coward!"

Crystal was smiling now, but still silent. A cloud of her cigarette smoke rose above her head. She was gloating, and had she known that it would have had such an impact she would have made it even better by tormenting Lena a little longer before killing her. She was gloating profusely now, and it was showing in her eyes. She was at the peak of her pride. She had killed her daughter. The intense pride lifted up her spirit and made her feel worth something.

Jim, for a third and final time slipped to his knees and wept over Lena's body. The sirens were wailing at State Road 84 now. He lapped his tongue at the salty blood streaking Lena's face. Then he suddenly stopped his crying and straightened. That was when he noticed the gathering crowd of curious people who were enjoying the excitement. He wiped away his tears and stood, his left hand resting on Crystal's shoulder. Would she let him stay close to her? If not, he would run her down. He stealthily slid his right hand into his pants pocket and gripped a heavy pocketknife. He pulled it out and flicked open the long, rusty blade. Jim turned before Crystal knew what was happening and sank the sharp blade to its hilt into her chest. He held on savagely to the knife, laughing hysterically. She gasped and twisted simultaneously and the blade snapped off inside of her. Jim moved back with the handle in his hand. He watched her collapse to the road and die in front of the growing crowd; the burning cigarette clung to her mouth.

A police car wailed through the intersection and roared to the scene with its siren echoing. Two cops leaped out and hurried forward.

Jim heard the crowd telling the cops that they were a second too late. Then he started stomping on Crystal's face. The cops rushed him with guns drawn. Jim only laughed and kept stomping on Crystal. Her front teeth were gone and her nose was smashed. One cop pulled the hammer back on his gun and put it to Jim's head, as he started stomping on her face again and laughing. Still attached to its string, one of Crystal's green eyes popped out and rolled to the road, and Jim started stomping on that too. Then the cop fired a shot next to his face and Jim froze, his desire to die vanishing as quickly as it had come. He looked down at Crystal's lifeless form as his arms were twisted behind his back and handcuffed. He too had won. He was ecstatic even though Lena was dead and he would spend the rest of his life in prison. It was well worth it. Crystal had played the game of cat and mouse with the wrong cat, and got eaten. Jim could not believe it. Only moments away from leaving her abusive mother, the nightmare of her life had come. Death had struck her down without warning. He still could not believe it. It was so sudden and so swift and thorough. Lena had lived and died for nothing. His soul, spirit and mind died with Lena's body. He had descended into the depths of hell. His sad eyes turned to his daughter's corpse and he knew that this was child abuse in the eyes of a child.